"I won't le██████████████ strayed to her mouth and her pulse jumped.

No matter that they shared a son, Drew was the kind of man she didn't want to be involved with, but the fact that he stirred her blood with just a look worried Hallie.

Before she did something she'd regret—like allow him to kiss her—she whispered, "Don't."

"Don't what?"

"Don't look like you want to kiss me," she whispered.

"Why?"

"Because."

"You'll have to come up with a better reason than *because*." His big, callused hand cupped her jaw. Then his mouth crushed hers, trapping the air in her lungs.

A hint of aftershave clung to his skin, and she nuzzled her nose against his cheek, greedily inhaling his scent. Her body had not forgotten him or his touch.

Dear Reader,

Rodeo Daddy kicks off my new series for the Harlequin American Romance line—Rodeo Rebels. The original version of this story was written more than ten years ago, before I sold my first book. The story collected its share of rejections, but I could never bring myself to toss it out. I'm glad I didn't. After much rewriting and guidance from my editor, *Rodeo Daddy* is ready for publication.

The inspiration for this story came about after vacationing with my family out West. I attended the Cheyenne Frontier Days Rodeo in Cheyenne, Wyoming. I remember the announcer introducing one of the cowboys who had suffered several mishaps prior to that night's rodeo. I wondered what would make a cowboy continue to compete with painful injuries. That *wondering* inspired this story.

Drew Rawlins is past his prime by rodeo standards but won't hang up his spurs until he's achieved what most cowboys never do—a world title. Drew will let nothing and no one stand in his way—especially his recent rib injury. Then Drew runs into Hallie—a woman he's never been able to forget—and learns their one-night stand five years ago resulted in a child. Juggling rodeo, fatherhood and his feelings for the mother of his son tests Drew's concentration and his commitment to his goal. I hope you enjoy traveling the rocky road of rodeo with Drew and Hallie as they struggle to find a way to be a family.

For more information on my books and other Rodeo Rebels stories visit www.marinthomas.com.

Cowboy up!

Marin

Rodeo Daddy

MARIN THOMAS

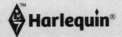

Harlequin®

TORONTO NEW YORK LONDON
AMSTERDAM PARIS SYDNEY HAMBURG
STOCKHOLM ATHENS TOKYO MILAN MADRID
PRAGUE WARSAW BUDAPEST AUCKLAND

Recycling programs
for this product may
not exist in your area.

ISBN-13: 978-0-373-75356-7

RODEO DADDY

Copyright © 2011 by Brenda Smith-Beagley

www.eHarlequin.com

Printed in U.S.A.

ABOUT THE AUTHOR

Marin Thomas grew up in Janesville, Wisconsin. She attended the University of Arizona in Tucson on a Division I basketball scholarship. In 1986, she graduated with a B.A. in radio-television and married her college sweetheart in a five-minute ceremony in Las Vegas. Marin was inducted in May 2005 into the Janesville Sports Hall of Fame for her basketball accomplishments. Even though she now calls Chicago home, she's a living testament to the old adage "You can take the girl out of the small town, but you can't take the small town out of the girl." Marin's heart still lies in small-town life, which she loves to write about in her books.

Books by Marin Thomas

HARLEQUIN AMERICAN ROMANCE

*The McKade Brothers
**Hearts of Appalachia

To Georgi—a great mother-in-law, casino-nickel-slot queen, world traveler and bargain hunter extraordinaire, whose favorite sayings include… "Save your money," "Shop in your closet" and "Be thankful you have a job."

Chapter One

"The Bastrop Homecoming Rodeo must be a hell of an event. You're the third cowboy today who's fallen off his horse."

Drew Rawlins glared at the E.R. doctor as he sucked in a lungful of sterilized air. Not smart. A burning band of pain squeezed his injured ribs, and the words escaped his mouth in a long wheeze. "I was *bucked* off."

"I'm Dr. Feller." The doctor flipped on the light box mounted against the wall and studied Drew's X-ray.

Drew prayed he wouldn't draw another crazed bronc like Demon the day after tomorrow when he competed in the final round of the saddle bronc competition. He'd been lucky today to escape with a kick to the chest.

"Your ribs are badly bruised. I recommend taking a few weeks off before you ride again."

Drew broke out in a sweat that had nothing to do with pain. In order to make the National Finals Rodeo in December, he needed to be among the top fifteen saddle bronc riders in the country. Today was August sixth—he was running out of time.

"You've got callus new bone formations on five of

your ribs." The doctor pointed to several spots on the X-ray.

So he'd fractured a few ribs over the years—Drew had fared better than most cowboys who'd competed at the sport as long as he had.

"You're lucky you didn't break a rib."

"I don't need luck, Doc." Drew chuckled, then winced as a flash of fiery pain snaked around his middle.

"Rib injuries are nothing to joke about." Feller leaned against the wall. "A fractured rib can puncture a lung, liver, spleen or worse."

Worse. The word sent a shiver down Drew's spine. He'd been ten years old when the famous bull rider Lane Frost had died at the Cheyenne Frontier Days Rodeo. After Frost had ridden Taking Care of Business and dismounted, the bull had turned and hit him in the side with one of his horns, breaking the cowboy's ribs. Frost had gotten up and headed toward the chutes, but had stumbled. When he'd hit the ground, a broken rib had severed his pulmonary artery, ending his life.

"Keep testing fate, cowboy, and you'll die with a mouthful of dirt or end up connected to a ventilator the rest of your life." The doctor waved his hand in the air. "Either way, the horse comes out the winner."

The solemn warning spawned another flashback.... Drew struggled to block out today's eight-second ride, but the image of the crazed gelding's hoof coming at him while he lay unprotected in the dirt had been branded on his brain.

"No worries. I don't plan to let another bronc stand on my chest." Drew was thirty-two. No longer in the prime of his life in the world of rodeo. He'd been bustin' broncs for fourteen years. If he ever had a chance at becoming a world champion, this was the year.

He needed the damned title to prove his dead father wrong—that Drew Rawlins hadn't wasted half his life chasing a dream. His father had been a rising star in bareback riding when he'd gotten Drew's mother pregnant. In order to support Drew and his mother, his father had given up rodeo and helped manage his father-in-law's small-town grocery store. To this day Drew believed his father had resented him because having a family had kept the old man from achieving his dream of making it to the NFR.

When Drew had graduated from high school and announced he intended to ride the circuit, his father had scoffed, insisting Drew didn't have what it took to be a champion. Drew ignored the old man, his focus solely on winning the granddaddy of 'em all. But the big one had eluded him. Drew had made it to the NFR the year his father had died—a decade ago—but he'd placed last. Last wasn't near good enough. Most cowboys with half a brain would have retired by now, but Drew had never forgotten his father's dying words before the cancer had taken him.

You ain't never gonna be as good as I was.

Angry at himself for allowing the memory to resurface, Drew inched closer to the edge of the examining table. He had plenty of experience with injured ribs. As long as he moved carefully and took shallow breaths, he could tolerate the pain.

"No rodeos for three weeks." Dr. Feller scribbled on a pad of paper.

Drew kept his mouth shut. Bruised ribs would not

prevent him from competing in the final go-round on Sunday. He needed the thousand-dollar jackpot to boost his earnings.

The doctor handed him a prescription. "For pain."

Pain was good. If he focused on the pain, there would be no room in his head for his father's taunts. "My boots are missing," he said, after spotting his shirt, which he'd thrown across the chair in the corner.

Ignoring Drew, the doctor rambled on. "You have a chance of developing pneumonia after a rib trauma. Take deep breaths and cough every hour to keep your lungs clear. An ice pack will help you feel more comfortable." He handed Drew his shirt.

"Does a nurse by the name of Hallie Sutton work here?" Drew clenched his teeth against the heat searing his side when he slid his arm into the shirtsleeve.

"How do you know Ms. Sutton?"

Ms. Hallie hadn't married? "She put a dozen stitches in my head five years ago."

Every year Drew competed in the Bastrop Homecoming Rodeo. And each time he searched for Hallie in the stands. Once, he'd driven to the hospital to look her up but had chickened out at the last minute and left town.

Just because you've never forgotten your one night with her doesn't mean she hasn't.

He remembered walking into Cozie's bar and spotting Hallie sitting at a table with her coworkers. When their gazes met, he'd been struck by the sadness in her brown eyes and had wondered what had happened to the cheerful, talkative nurse who'd stitched his head earlier in the afternoon. The abject misery reflected in

Hallie's expression had drawn him to her. Before he'd realized his actions, he'd asked her to dance. At first, she'd refused, then at the prodding of her friends she'd allowed him to lead her onto the dance floor. Drew closed his eyes as the memory swept him away....

"Want to talk about it?" he'd whispered in Hallie's ear.

"No." She'd burrowed into him as if seeking protection from whatever had tormented her.

He'd held her close and they'd danced forever—at least eight songs. Then the band had taken a break and so had Hallie's friends—they'd left the bar. "Need a lift home?"

"I don't want to go home." Her brown eyes had shimmered with tears.

"We could keep dancing," he'd offered.

"No."

"Hungry?"

"No."

"Wanna talk?"

"Not here."

"C'mon." He'd grabbed her hand and led her outside. The August night had been warm and muggy. "There's a coffee shop down the road." When she hadn't taken him up on the suggestion he'd thrown caution to the wind. "My camper's parked a few blocks away. We could talk there."

Hallie had stared at him for the longest time before she'd slipped her arm through his. "Okay."

The one word had sent Drew's blood thundering through his veins. They'd walked in silence, Drew preparing for anything once they reached the camper—anything except Hallie jumping his bones as soon as they'd stepped inside.

Twice, he'd attempted to take the high road and put a stop to her advances. Hallie might not have been drunk, but she hadn't been herself, either. He'd been no match for her persistence. Her touches and kisses had been edged with desperation, and her urgency fueled his desire for her. Their union had been as combustible as a four-alarm fire.

"These will hold you over until you fill the prescription." The doctor held out two pain pills and a Dixie cup of water.

"Thanks." Drew tossed back the medicine.

"If you suffer nausea, dizziness or have trouble breathing—"

"I know the routine."

The noise out of Feller's mouth sounded like the snort a bull gave when a cowboy settled onto its back. Shaking his head, the doctor left the cubicle, white coat tails flapping in his wake.

Drew closed his eyes and focused on the pain. Pain, he could handle.

Giving up rodeo, he could not.

HALLIE SUTTON stepped through the emergency doors of Lakeside Hospital and squinted until her eyes adjusted to the bright fluorescent lights. Aside from a muffled grunt drifting into the hallway, the E.R. appeared quiet. Her best friend and mentor, Sharon, manned the nurses' station.

"Thanks for filling in on short notice." Sharon's

orange corkscrew curls bounced around her head as she spoke.

"Sure." Hallie locked her purse in a cabinet drawer. "Who's the lucky nurse?" She sniffed a bouquet of red roses on the counter.

"No one. A patient checked out this morning and left them behind. Our station was next on the list for free flowers." Sharon gestured over her shoulder. "Look who's heading this way."

Dr. Mark Feller—the newest doctor on staff.

For two months Mark had pestered Hallie for a date. This past Friday she'd agreed to dinner and a movie. The evening had gone well until he'd kissed her good-night. No sparks. No tingly, fuzzy feelings. Nothing. She blamed her inability to respond to the handsome blond-haired man on a certain cowboy from her past. A cowboy she should have forgotten years ago.

"Hallie. What are you doing here?" Mark's eyes never left her face as he handed Sharon a medical chart. Hallie caught a whiff of his designer cologne—the light lime scent would be the nicest odor she smelled all day.

"I'm filling in for Liz," Hallie said. "Her daughter has the chicken pox."

Mark winked. "Call me when you break for dinner and I'll meet you in the cafeteria." He walked to the elevator bank and punched the button, then faced Hallie. "The guy in…" Mark's pager bleeped. After checking the number he switched directions and disappeared down the corridor, Hallie forgotten.

"What's he like in bed?"

"I haven't slept with him." Hallie hadn't had sex in, well, since…never mind.

"Not for lack of trying on the good doctor's part, I'm sure."

Hallie arranged the charts on the counter and ignored the heat suffusing her neck. Sharon was right. During their date, Mark had made it clear—in a teasing way—that he was physically attracted to her and wouldn't turn down an invitation to join her in bed. Although Mark was a nice man, like most of the doctors she worked with, he was married to his career. Hallie didn't want a fling. She wanted forever. As for a one-night stand with Mark... She'd made that mistake once and it had changed her life forever.

"You're twenty-eight years old, Hallie." Sharon's eyes twinkled. "Age is progressive, not regressive."

"Thanks for the reminder." Hallie examined her reflection in the shiny metal supply cabinet. She couldn't do anything about her generous bust line, but she was proud of her flat tummy. Her hips were a bit curvy—she blamed it on her short stature. She flipped her blond braid over her shoulder. Hmm... Maybe a new hairstyle. Oh, who was she kidding? She barely arrived to work on time after getting herself and her son ready for the day.

"Dr. Feller's handsome. Successful. Sexy." Sharon bumped her aside and opened the cabinet. "What's holding you back?"

Successful and handsome—Dr. Mark Feller in a nutshell. But Mark wasn't interested in a long-term relationship and his kiss had left her cold. Hallie had felt the fire once in her life. Why should she settle for anything less?

"C'mon," Sharon teased. "Jump in with both feet."

The last time Hallie had jumped, she'd darn near drowned. She wasn't about to leap again—not in this lifetime.

"Hey! Anyone out there? I need my damned boots!"

Hallie chuckled and looked at Sharon.

"Some cowpoke from the rodeo. Bruised ribs." Sharon perused the patient's paperwork. "Prescribed pain meds and advised against competing for three weeks." She closed the chart and handed it to Hallie. "Patient refused doctor advice."

"Typical." Rodeo cowboys weren't short on guts, but they were missing half their brains.

"Discharge him before he tears the place apart." Sharon grabbed a pair of dusty ropers from beneath the counter. "They were left in the ambulance. An off-duty paramedic brought them in a few minutes ago."

A pungent odor permeated the shabby boots, and Hallie crinkled her nose. Judging by the worn-down heels and decaying leather, they should have been discarded years ago.

Boots in hand Hallie marched down the hall, then flung aside the cubicle curtain. "Besides your—" The ropers escaped her grasp and thudded against the floor. A loud buzzing filled her ears, and her chest constricted until she feared she'd drawn her last breath.

Drew. Hallie felt the blood drain from her face, then rush back with such force her head throbbed.

"Been a long time, Hallie."

The mellow drawl sailed across the room and smacked her in the chest, jarring her out of her stupor.

After five long years, his voice—its deep pitch, the husky endearment—sounded all too familiar.

Drew's brow wrinkled with concern. "Hey, you okay?"

No, she was not okay. Her life was on the verge of crumbling, yet all her stupid heart could do was pitter-patter over the cowboy's good looks and sexy voice. "I'm fine."

She surreptitiously studied Drew while pretending to read his chart. He looked older. Harder. More intimidating than she'd remembered. His eyes bore the brunt of aging, the once bright blue irises had faded and were glazed with pain.

Sympathy welled up inside her, until she reminded herself that since their one night together, her life had been no walk in the park, either.

He hadn't buttoned his shirt and when he caught her staring at his muscular pecs, he grinned. White teeth pulled her attention from the squint lines around his eyes to his shaggy hair and the few strands of silver mixed with dark brown at his temples. One thing for certain, aging hadn't affected the man's sex appeal.

"Mind handing me those?" He pointed to the floor.

She thrust the boots at him.

"Thanks."

While he tugged the ancient ropers over his dingy athletic socks, she noticed his shaking hands and rapid breathing. Her nursing instincts kicked in. Placing her fingers against his wrist, she forced herself to concentrate on the second hand of her watch.

His scent surrounded her—a mixture of sweat, dust and faded aftershave. Everything about this man was so…male and earthy. His bronzed hand—large, strong and covered in calluses—brought back memories of his leather-tough caresses. "Your pulse is a little fast." The mulish man needed rest.

"That's because you're standing so close." The words teased, but his eyes were stone-cold sober.

Had she ever crossed Drew's mind through the years the way he'd drifted in and out of hers? Hallie would never forget the day she'd met him in the emergency room, or the phone call she'd received hours later informing her that her foster mother had passed away. Hallie often wondered if it had been fate or destiny that had brought Drew into the bar later that evening.

In Drew's arms she'd forgotten her pain. Forgotten for a brief time that she'd been all alone in the world. But reality had sunk in when she'd awoken in the wee hours of the morning and realized she'd slept with a cowboy. Until Drew, Hallie had managed to avoid cowboys. Her father had taught her that cowboys only cared about themselves and not others. Before the break of day, Hallie had left the camper and returned to her apartment, feeling more alone than she'd ever felt before.

"Do you always sneak out after having sex with a man?" Drew asked.

Tamping down the panic building inside her, she ignored the question and passed him the clipboard. "After you sign these papers, you're free to go."

They locked gazes, before he scribbled his signature. "I left messages for you at the hospital."

Six messages to be exact. Six notes begging her to call him. She'd tossed them into the trash, convinced that ignoring Drew had been the best course of action.

Drew stood...slowly. His body dwarfed her five-foot-six frame, his shoulders blocking the view of the hallway. His stare sent her stomach into a nosedive.

"Unless I don't remember right, you enjoyed yourself as much as I did." His eyes dared her to deny the truth.

For a few hours Drew had made Hallie forget the heartache of losing her foster mother. In the end, their brief time together had left her tied to Drew in a way no one, not even the cowboy, knew. "Is there someone to take care of you?" The question was purely professional.

Yeah, right.

"There's no special woman in my life." He grinned. "If that's what you're asking."

Heat crawled up her neck as she tore off a copy of the discharge papers. Drew Rawlins toyed with fate. Spit into the wind. A cowboy hell-bent on suicide. What cruel twist of fate brought the man back to this hospital, stirring up painful memories and guilt?

"You're the best judge of how you feel," she said. "If the pain worsens, you have trouble breathing or run a fever, seek medical help right away."

He lifted his dusty, seen-better-days Stetson from the examining table and settled it on his head. Drew had come a long way from the cowboy who'd danced with her, consoled her, then bedded her.

"I'll be riding in the saddle-bronc competition Sunday afternoon." He paused. "I'll leave a ticket at Will Call."

"You shouldn't—"

"Busting broncs is in my blood, beautiful." His brazen smile set off warning bells in her head.

In spite of bruised ribs, he planned to compete in two days. Only a man whose whole life was rodeo would take such a risk. She considered the choices she'd made in the past, and relief filled her. Drew Rawlins didn't want or need anyone. "Thanks, but I have plans."

His expression turned thoughtful. "My loss. Again." The sound of his clomping boots echoed down the hall and, in Hallie's memory, through the rest of her shift and long into the night.

"YOU HEADING OUT to the bars with the rest of us?"

Drew shook his head. Brody Murphy was the closest thing to a best friend Drew had. "Not tonight."

"How bad is it? You riding Sunday?" Brody eased the red Dodge truck away from the hospital emergency entrance.

"Bruised ribs. I'm riding." Like every cowboy worth his salt, Drew had ridden injured more times than he cared to remember.

"You sure that's smart?"

"What do you know about being smart?" Brody was the worst bull rider Drew had met in ages. The man's longest ride this season had lasted five seconds. Brody had joined the circuit two years ago and hadn't improved much. When Drew had asked why he continued to ride bulls when he sucked at the sport, Brody had confessed that the sport helped keep his mind off his dead daughter and ex-wife.

"Something happen in that E.R. aside from a few X-rays?" Brody asked.

Yeah. *Hallie* had happened. At first, Drew believed she hadn't changed much. She wore her hair the same as the first time he'd laid eyes on her—in a long, honey-colored braid. And her figure had been as stacked as he'd remembered, maybe even a little fuller in all the right places. He'd noticed a subtle difference in her face, more specifically her eyes. The glistening brown color reminded him of well-oiled saddle leather, but the once welcoming warmth had been guarded, wary.

"You got a dreamy look on your face, hoss." Brody batted his eyelashes like a street-corner hooker.

Drew chuckled, then groaned. "I ran into an old acquaintance."

"What's the scoop on this *acquaintance* who caught your eye?"

"She's pretty." *Pretty edgy.* Hallie had acted skittish as a horse in a barn full of fighting cats. The whole encounter had left Drew's gut tied in knots.

"How pretty?" Rodeo groupies followed Brody everywhere—not because of his bull-riding success. His movie-star face and compact muscular body had earned him the nickname Hollywood. Brody pretended to enjoy the spotlight, but Drew knew it was an act. At the end of the night the bull rider left the bars alone.

"She's blonde. Petite. Brown eyes. Nice body." *No wedding ring.*

"Ask her out."

"I invited her to the rodeo Sunday."

"And…?"

"She declined." Drew's chest ached more from wounded pride than bruised ribs.

"Too bad."

Hallie's message had been loud and clear—she'd rather treat herself to a new pair of shoes than another steamy go-round in bed with him.

"Maybe she'll show." Brody turned into a trailer park at the edge of town. Fifty or so campers sat parked haphazardly in the gravel lot. There were no trees, only scraggly bushes and weeds poking through the gravel. Empty beer bottles and garbage littered the ground.

"You make more money at this sport than most cowboys. Why don't you invest in a decent place to live?" Brody parked in front of Drew's beat-up camper.

The trailer-truck might not be the newest model, but the heap of junk was paid for. Most of his winnings went toward fixing up the small ranch he'd purchased a year ago with the money he'd inherited from the sale of his grandfather's grocery store. Besides, he liked his privacy. He'd quit sharing motel rooms with his competition years ago. "If I win in Vegas, I'll hang up my spurs for good and burn the damned piece of crap."

"I heard Fitzgerald jawing about you behind the chutes today."

Riley Fitzgerald was a black-haired, blue-eyed hotheaded college grad, who happened to have the luck of the Irish on his side. Drew first met Fitzgerald at cowboy camp, where Drew had been hired to give bronc-riding lessons to rich kids. Fitzgerald had been in Drew's group and the seventeen-year-old had been a pain in the ass—always bragging and challenging Drew to ride-offs. When the camp had ended, Fitzgerald had boasted that Drew had better watch out because one day he'd beat him.

Later that year Drew had heard Fitzgerald was heading to the University of Nevada at Las Vegas to bust broncs in college. The kid had ended up winning the national championship his senior year. As soon as he'd graduated from college, Fitzgerald had hit the rodeo circuit. Now three years later the pain in the ass was a favorite to win the NFR in December.

"I don't listen to gossip," Drew said.

Brody's face sobered. "The guy's good."

Most cowboys didn't have the privilege of being raised in a wealthy family or having all their entry fees and traveling expenses covered. Hell, Fitzgerald flew to rodeos all over the country in a private jet paid for by his father. Even so, Drew held one advantage over the Irishman—he had more at stake. "I'm not worried." Drew hopped out of the truck and gingerly shut the door. "See you tomorrow."

Once inside his cramped home-on-wheels, Drew stretched out on the sleeper bed above the front seats. As soon as he closed his eyes, his mind drifted back five years.... The afternoon he'd gone to the hospital for stitches in his head. Snatches of images and sensations—the gentle touch of fingers against his skull, a soft, feminine voice—prevented him from falling asleep.

Hallie.

In the quiet darkness, Drew let down his guard and admitted that running into Hallie had been bittersweet. He'd always believed their one night together had been magical. Seeing her after all these years made him feel as if he'd missed out on something special.

What's done is done. After Sunday's competition he'd leave Bastrop and his memories of Hallie behind.

For good this time.

Chapter Two

Late Sunday afternoon a gust of wind plastered Hallie's hair to her face, temporarily blinding her as she hurried after her four-year-old son. "Nicholas, slow down!"

A few hours ago she'd found a note in Nick's backpack. The preschool teacher needed chaperones next Thursday for an outing to the well-known Roscar's Chocolate shop. Hallie had promised Nick they'd stop by the hospital to see if one of the nurses would swap shifts with her so she could accompany him on the field trip.

"Hurry, Mom."

Since the moment he'd learned to walk, Nick went about life at a hundred miles per hour regardless of the risks. She worried about her son's fearlessness—a trait he hadn't inherited from her. There was only one time Hallie had gone with her instincts, let her mind shut down and allowed her body and soul to— *Never again.*

Following a couple of sleepless nights, plagued with visions of Drew Rawlins flying off a crazed horse, Hallie had woken angry with herself for worrying whether the bull-headed Texan was tough enough to survive another ride. After today's rodeo competition Drew would move on. Out of town. Out of her life. *Out of her mind.*

The E.R. doors suddenly whooshed open. "Nick, watch out!"

The warning came too late. Her son's forehead smacked against the man's belt buckle. He grabbed Nick's shoulder to steady him. "What's the hurry, squirt?"

The familiar voice shocked Hallie clear down to her toes. *Drew?*

Nick rubbed his forehead. "That hurt."

"No doubt, pardner. There's a big ol' stallion branded between your eyes."

Please, God. Don't let him discover the truth. Fear pressed against Hallie's chest as she bit her bottom lip, the coppery tang of blood seeping into her mouth. "Hello, Drew."

Startled, Drew glanced up. "Hallie?" His gaze swung between her and Nick.

The doors opened again. Another cowboy, his arm in a sling, stopped next to Drew. Shorter than Drew by several inches, the broad-shouldered man had sandy blond hair, a deep tan and a killer smile. He looked more like an actor than a rodeo cowboy.

Nick wiggled free and chased after a cricket hopping along the sidewalk. A fierce surge of protectiveness forced aside Hallie's anxiety. "Did you reinjure your ribs?"

"Ribs are fine." Drew nodded to the other man. "Brody busted his wrist."

"I'm sorry to hear that."

"No need to feel bad for me, ma'am. I've survived worse." The cowboy's smile didn't reach his eyes.

Drew watched Hallie. She acted nervous. He told himself it didn't matter, but he hoped her job was the reason she'd missed seeing him outride Fitzgerald a short time ago. His earnings today advanced him to sixteenth place. "On your way to work?" he asked.

"Running errands." Her long blond hair flowing over her shoulders, Drew was taken aback by her pouty lips and big brown eyes. Hallie was by far the most memorable woman he'd ever known.

She made a move to step past him, but he shuffled sideways, blocking her path. Her face paled and the hairs on the back of Drew's neck stood on end.

Two days ago Hallie had made him feel worthless as green slime in a horse trough. Normally, he loved a good challenge, but he was smart enough to realize when the odds weren't in his favor. He cursed the fates that had brought this woman into his life five years ago. He should have stowed Hallie on the shelf of experience—way in the back. Instead, he'd spent the years since their night together taking her down and dusting off her memory. *What a frickin' waste of time.*

"Let's go, Nick."

"Look, Mom. I'm an airplane." The boy ran in circles with his arms extended, sputtering engine sounds.

The kid was her son? Drew's stomach clenched as if he'd been sucker punched. He'd thought of Hallie a lot over the years—just never as a mother.

The airplane landed next to Drew. "Hey, mister. Are you a real cowboy?"

Eyes on Hallie, Drew said, "I'm as real as they come."

"I'm gonna be a cowboy when I grow up."

Drew spared the boy a quick glance. "Gonna ride bulls or broncs?"

"What's a bronc?"

"A bucking horse."

"What do you ride?"

"Broncs." Drew watched Hallie's reaction, but her stoic face gave no clue how she felt about his chosen career.

"Bulls are meaner and tougher," Brody whispered.

"I'm gonna ride broncs," the boy said.

Brody scoffed. "Why?"

The boy pointed to Drew's waist. "His buckle's bigger 'n yours."

Red-faced, Brody said, "I'll wait in the truck."

When Hallie grabbed the little guy's arm, Drew noticed her bare ring finger, which meant nothing. She probably had a man in her life. He envied the lucky son of a gun who'd won her heart. "How old are you?" he asked the boy.

"I'm—"

"Nick!" Hallie's tortured expression sucked the air from Drew's lungs. "We're in a hurry."

She hadn't acted this nervous when he'd invited her into his camper all those years ago. Puzzled, he asked, "What's the matter?"

"Nothing." She sounded out of breath. "Why?"

"You're jumpier than a—" Hallie shifted sideways, and Drew got his first good look at the boy. He scrambled to fit the pieces together....

Hallie's nervousness.

Cutting her son off before he could tell Drew how old he was.

Trying to rush the boy inside the hospital.

Holy crap. Was the kid his?

He willed his mind to fabricate a plausible explanation, but his thoughts became entangled—waking up buck-naked on the bed, the blankets in a twisted heap on the floor. The lingering scent of Hallie's perfume permeating the sheets. The two condoms he'd always kept in his wallet...*still there*.

No goodbye. No note. Just gone.

Shock switched to anger, its talons sinking into his flesh and twisting, until he felt physically ill. He was a father—had been a father for the past few years without ever realizing. Whether or not Hallie wanted him involved in their son's life, Drew had a right to know a part of himself existed out there in the world.

"Is there something you need to tell me?"

The color drained from Hallie's face, leaving her skin pasty white. She clasped her son's hand and stepped toward the doors.

"Wait." Drew knelt in front of the boy. "Your name's Nick?"

"Uh-huh."

He leveled a cool stare at Hallie, daring her to deny what he suspected. Not only did Nick inherit his strong jaw, but the boy's eyes were also close in color to Drew's. He waited for an explanation—half of him wishing she'd admit he was the boy's father, the other half wishing he'd never fallen victim to Hallie's sad eyes the night he'd stumbled upon her at Cozie's bar.

With a trembling hand she brushed the hair from her face. The urge to hug her was automatic, but Drew shoved aside the feeling and stomped it flat. How a decent, sweet young woman could do such a thing baffled him.

"Hallie?" *Speak, damn it.* The idea of a single night of loving turning into a lifetime commitment scared Drew more than the kick in the ribs he'd suffered on Friday. The timing couldn't be worse. Did he skip his next rodeo and stay in town to…to…what?

The E.R. doors opened and Hallie pulled Nick to the side. Drew recognized the nurse—the same woman who had checked him into the emergency room two days earlier. She paused when she noticed him. He nodded, but was spared from speaking to her when she spotted Hallie and Nick.

"What are you two doing here?" the nurse asked.

"Hi, Aunt Sharon," Nick said. "Mom's gonna see if she can go on my field trip to the candy store."

"That sounds like fun." Aunt Sharon frowned at Drew. "Everything okay, Hallie?"

Hallie's eyes begged Drew to walk away.

He shook his head. He wasn't leaving until he got the answers he deserved.

Aunt Sharon must have sensed the tension between Hallie and Drew, because she grasped Nick's hand. "Come with me. We just filled the candy dish at the nurses' station."

"I'll be right in," Hallie said. Once Nick left with Aunt Sharon, Hallie retreated to a shady spot a short distance from the door. Drew followed.

"Why didn't you tell me?" He was surprised his voice sounded so civil when his insides rioted.

Hallie's eyes watered, but her tears only angered him. "I enter the Bastrop rodeo every year," he said. "You could have contacted the local rodeo commissioner. He would have gotten word to me that you wanted to meet." Drew removed his hat and tunneled his fingers through his hair. "Hell, Hallie. For four years I've been a father—" the word filled Drew with pride, but the feeling lasted only seconds before fear took over "—and I hadn't a clue."

"I can't do this," she whispered. "Not here."

Anger and relief warred inside Drew. Anger that Hallie was calling the shots and relief he wouldn't have to face the past right now. He needed time to digest the bombshell she'd dropped on him. "I'm heading to Oklahoma." He winced at the cool note in his voice. He hadn't meant to sound uncaring, but the sooner he put distance between him and Hallie the better.

As if she'd been holding her breath the whole time, the air escaped her mouth in a loud whoosh. "Good luck with your next rodeo." No mistaking the silent message behind her words. Hallie Sutton wanted nothing from him.

That pissed him off.

She skirted past him and entered the hospital. Fearing he might run after her, he spun and headed across the parking lot.

"Oooweee!" Brody grinned when Drew hopped into his buddy's truck. "She the nurse you ran into on Friday?"

"Yep."

"You get a date out of her?"

"I got more than a date from her." Drew expected the words to come easy, but they damn near choked him. "She gave me a son."

Brody's mouth dropped open. "Jeez, hoss. That was your kid back there?"

"Yeah. Hallie and I had a one-night stand five years ago." Her touches…kisses…whispers in his ear had made him forget his goal—rodeo.

Even now, the anger churning in his gut competed with the rush of attraction lingering in his veins. His body refused to forget how Hallie had filled his arms… and for one night had filled his heart.

"What's the kid's name?"

"Nick." Why had Hallie kept their son a secret? To Drew's way of thinking, there wasn't any excuse in the world that made such a lie okay.

"Oh, hell." Drew clenched his hands. Fatherhood had never been in his plans. Acknowledging his responsibility to his son—easy. Handling the responsibility— ball-busting. He'd always fallen short in his father's eyes. There was no guarantee his son wouldn't find him just as lacking. Dragging his hands down his face, Drew sucked in a deep breath. Then another. And another. Until his ribs burned.

A cold sweat broke out across his brow. Although he resented being burdened with this new dilemma in the middle of rodeo season, this latest turn of events added a new dimension to his quest for the title—he wanted to win not only for himself, but also for his son. He wanted Nick to be proud to have him for a father.

And what about Hallie? Part of him—the part below

the belt buckle—still hungered for her. Each time he saw her would he want more? He couldn't afford to allow his attraction to her mess with his concentration. "What the hell am I supposed to do now?"

Brody shrugged. "Seems you gave the lady your answer when you let her walk away."

"HEY, MOM." Nick waved at Hallie from the nurses' station in the E.R. "Aunt Sharon gave me a sucker with a smiley face on it."

Hallie noticed Aunt Sharon wasn't smiling. She owed her friend an explanation. "Nick, why don't you watch TV in the lounge. I need to chat with Aunt Sharon a minute and then check to see if I can switch my shift next Thursday."

As soon as Nick skipped off, Sharon bombarded Hallie with questions. "Who was that cowboy? He looked familiar." Sharon snapped her fingers. "He was in the E.R. this past Friday."

"His name is Drew Rawlins. You might also remember him from the night my foster mother passed away."

Sharon whistled between her teeth. "That was the cowboy who asked you to dance at Cozie's?"

"Yes."

"You two did more than dance, didn't you?"

"Drew is Nick's father." Hallie had never told anyone until now.

"So the secret's finally out." Sharon glanced away but not before Hallie caught the look of hurt on her friend's face.

When Hallie had realized she was pregnant, Sharon

had asked who the father was and if he intended to be involved in the baby's life. Hallie was ashamed to admit she'd kept Drew's identity to herself and had insisted he'd wanted nothing to do with raising his child.

"You never told Drew you were pregnant all those years ago." It was a statement, not a question.

"No, I didn't." She supposed she should have confided in Sharon, but she'd feared no one would understand her reasons for keeping Nick a secret from his father.

"What happens next?" Sharon asked.

"I'm not sure." Hallie's throat tightened. The firm grasp she'd kept on her emotions since running into Drew began to loosen.

"He'll want to get to know Nick. I expect Drew has family who'll wish to meet—"

"I don't want to think about that," Hallie said. Drew was practically a stranger. She knew nothing about his personal life, and the idea of sharing her son with the cowboy scared her senseless. She and Nick had a nice life in Bastrop. She was happy with her job at the hospital. Nick was settled in at his preschool. They had each other and plenty of friends. Friends Hallie considered family. Nick didn't need Drew's relatives to fill any void in his life.

What about a father? Doesn't your son deserve a father?

Yes, but not one like Drew—not a cowboy whose only concern was rodeo.

"You have to tell Nick," Sharon said.

Maybe. Maybe not. Hallie would wait for Drew to make the next move. Hopefully his decision would lead him farther away, not closer to Bastrop.

EIGHT O'CLOCK. The setting sun cast long shadows across the lot outside the small apartment complex where Hallie and Nick lived. Parked in a visitor's stall, Drew rubbed his fist in the center of his chest. The achy, tight feeling hadn't eased any since earlier in the afternoon. He and Brody had left town, intent on making it to Lawton, Oklahoma, before stopping for a bite to eat. He'd driven ten miles, then signaled Brody to go on without him and Drew had returned to Bastrop.

He couldn't leave the area until he'd settled things with Hallie—even though he had no idea what *things* needed settling.

A loud tap on the window startled him. A wrinkled face pressed against the glass. "Young man." *Tap. Tap.* "Young man."

Drew cracked the window six inches, afraid the old biddy might clobber him on the head with her cane. "Yes, ma'am?"

"You don't look like you're from around here. Are you one of those stalkers?"

"No, ma'am, I'm not a stalker."

She frowned, her rheumy eyes vanishing in the wrinkled folds of her face. "You a child molester?"

"No, ma'am. I am not a child molester."

"Get out here so I can get a better look at ya." She backed up a few steps.

Slowly, Drew got out of the camper. He towered over the old woman.

She pointed her cane at him. "What business brings you to these apartments?"

"That's private, ma'am."

"You've been parked here for a half hour."

So the old woman had been watching him. "Gathering my courage."

"Courage for what?"

"To speak to your neighbor."

"Who might that be?"

The nosy woman both amused and annoyed Drew. "I didn't catch your name, ma'am."

"Miss Rose. I was a school teacher in Bastrop for forty years. I know everyone who lives in these apartments. What's your name?"

"Drew Rawlins."

"The name don't sound familiar. You best mosey along."

"I'm here to see Hallie Sutton."

"I taught Hallie in seventh grade. That girl—" the rubber tip of the cane poked Drew in the chest "—knows better than to waste her time on a drifter."

"I don't drift, Miss Rose. I rodeo."

"Same difference."

Drew swallowed a chuckle. "I believe it's up to Hallie to decide if she's wasting her time on me or not."

"Watch that sharp tongue, young man." Miss Rose jabbed her cane, but Drew sidestepped and the rubber tip thunked the camper window.

"Have a nice evening, Miss Rose." Drew tipped his hat, then headed toward Apartment 9. Obtaining Hallie's address hadn't been difficult. After returning to town, he'd gone to the hospital and used his cowboy charm on the receptionist in Admitting.

Drew loitered on Hallie's stoop, struggling to compose a speech—not an easy task when his emotions were a jumbled mess.

"Watcha waiting for?" Miss Rose called from the sidewalk. Damned old biddy wasn't going to leave him alone until she knew Hallie was safe. He rapped his knuckles against the door.

The scraping sound of a dead bolt met his ear. The door opened until the safety chain snapped taut. Hallie's big brown eyes peeked at him, then she gasped, the sound reminding him of an angry rattler.

"Go away."

I wish I could. "We need to talk."

"I have nothing to say to you."

Only the toe of his boot prevented her from shutting the door in his face. "We have an audience." Drew shifted so Hallie could see her neighbor.

"Do you know this man?" Miss Rose asked.

Indecision warred in Hallie's eyes for one second before she spoke. "Yes, Miss Rose. Everything's fine."

The old woman wasn't convinced. She didn't budge from the sidewalk.

"You don't have to say a word. I'll do the talking," Drew said.

"Walk away, Drew. Please." Hallie's glance darted to her neighbor.

"I'll wait on the doorstep all night if I have to."

"You're not welcome here."

No kidding.

"I'll call the police," Hallie whispered.

Where did she get off being angry? If anyone deserved to be peeved, it was him. He was the innocent party, and he resented being treated like the villain.

He caught a glimpse of her bare foot poking the carpet inside the apartment. Five pedicured pink toenails spawned memories of legs tangling and… He cleared his throat. "I'd rather not air our dirty laundry in public."

"Say what you came to say, then leave." She thrust her chin in the air, her eyes wide and anxious.

She's scared.

Good. She ought to be after keeping his son a secret for five years. Drew couldn't get his head around the fact that he'd been a father all this time and hadn't known. "We can have this discussion right here, in front of Miss Rose."

Hallie's eyelids drifted shut in defeat. The door closed in his face, then reopened. He waved at the old biddy, then stepped into the apartment.

From across the room Hallie waited for Drew to secure the door locks. Before he had a chance to speak, Nick burst into the living room.

"Slow down," she warned as Nick zoomed past the sofa, his Batman cape swirling in the air. When he spotted their visitor, he applied the brakes.

Chest puffing, Nick stared wide-eyed. "I remember you."

Drew rolled the brim of his Stetson between his fingers and grinned. The man's smile was lethal. All these years, she'd blamed her reckless behavior on her foster mother's death. But seeing Drew again convinced her that no matter her state of mind that evening, she hadn't stood a chance against the cowboy's sex appeal and rakish charm.

Forget about your attraction to Drew. Focus on protecting Nick.

She gripped the back of the recliner until her knuckles turned white, and pain shot through her forearms.

She knew from personal experience that rodeo cowboys made terrible fathers.

Nick pointed to Drew's belt buckle. "Do you got lots of horses?"

"Not yet, but one day I plan to raise cutting horses."

"What's a cutting horse?"

"A horse that ranchers use to work cattle."

"Do you gotta ranch?"

"I do."

"Where is it?"

Hallie rubbed her brow. Nick didn't have a reputation as a chatter bug. He only asked questions if the subject piqued his interest. Interest was fine. But the undisguised wonder on her son's face right now scared the daylights out of her.

Over the past six months her little angel had sprouted horns. Nick had become combative with the kids at preschool. At home, he obeyed but only if she used threats. The awe in Nick's eyes as he ogled Drew confirmed her suspicion that her son's rude behavior was a cry for male attention.

"Dry Creek Acres is near a small town called Lakerville." Drew glanced at Hallie, his eyes dark with anger. "Not far from here."

That Drew had been relatively close to Bastrop all these years unnerved Hallie. She'd been a fool to believe she could raise their son without ever crossing paths with the cowboy.

"Can I see your ranch?"

"Enough questions, Nicholas. Go brush your teeth."

"But, I wanna—"

"Time for bed, young man."

"No." Nick stomped his foot on the carpet.

"Whoa there, pardner," Drew drawled in a terrible John Wayne impersonation, but he'd caught Nick's interest. "That ain't no way ta treat a lady." He softened the reprimand with a wink and her son morphed into a repenting angel.

Nick shuffled across the room. "Sorry."

Hallie sympathized with her son's need for a male role model, but her heart begged him not to choose the man standing in their living room. "Apology accepted."

"'Bye, mister!" Nick raced down the hallway.

"What I have to say, Hallie, may take a while." Drew's deep voice prompted a memory—tugging off boots, unbuttoning shirts, pushing denim over hips, whispered words… *"Relax, darlin'. This is gonna take a while."*

Good grief. She shook her head, embarrassed by the lustful thoughts. Drew was here because of their son, *not* because he hadn't been able to forget her.

"Let me check on Nick." Without waiting for a reply, she left the room, determined to gain the upper hand before the night ended.

Chapter Three

Drew glanced around Hallie's apartment. Muted shades of beige and navy colored the cramped living room. A TV occupied the middle shelf of a bookcase against the far wall. Keepsakes and photographs crowded the surrounding shelves. A snapshot of Hallie sporting a baby bump dragged him away from the door.

He ran a finger over the dusty frame, thinking the sadness in her eyes was at odds with her bright smile. The photo of Hallie pregnant—with his child—made everything *real*.

An empty feeling caught him by surprise. Hallie and Nick lived a full life. He suspected Hallie's career as a nurse allowed for plenty of friends and a busy social schedule. She was probably active in Nick's activities—whatever those were. Drew didn't know what his son's likes or dislikes were, what his favorite sport was, who took care of him when Hallie went to work. Drew felt like an outsider.

You are an outsider.

Drew's life consisted of rodeo and his dreams—winning the title and starting his horse ranch. Shoving the lonely ache aside, he took inventory of the room.

Plastic building blocks were scattered across the carpet next to a wicker basket filled with nursing magazines and medical journals. A pile of folded laundry sat on the end of the sofa. He resisted the temptation to check if the lacy pink strap peeking from beneath a towel was Hallie's bra.

Half-wilted wildflowers jammed into a vase rested on the sofa table. Had another man given them to Hallie? Nothing in the apartment hinted that an adult male lived there. No sports magazines, empty beer bottles or dirty socks lying around. The knowledge pleased him—not because of his attraction to Hallie, but because he didn't care for the idea of another man assuming Drew's role in Nick's life.

Hallie returned and walked past him without a word or glance. Not waiting for an invitation he followed her to the tiny kitchen and propped a shoulder against the door frame. Hands shoved into his pockets, he watched her fuss with the dirty cookware in the sink.

Tight jeans emphasized her curves—having a baby had softened the edges of her once svelte frame. Her faded pink T-shirt hugged her breasts, reminding him of a night he was better off forgetting. He guessed it was up to him to initiate conversation. Eyeing the dish towel on the counter, he asked, "Need a hand?"

"Sure." She edged sideways, making room for him at the sink. He caught her scent—faded perfume and a sweet almond smell from her hair. He breathed deeply and closed his eyes.

"What's the matter?" she asked.

"Nothing." Embarrassed that standing next to Hallie unnerved him, he dried a frying pan, then moved across the room to check out Nick's artwork on the refrigerator door. A picture of two stick figures in the bottom corner caught his eye. A tall one with yellow-marker hair and a short one with black-marker hair. *My family* was scrawled across the top of the paper. Once again a feeling of being left out doused him like a cold bucket of—

"Iced tea?" Hallie offered.

"No, thanks." He motioned to the kitchen doorway. "Is Nick asleep?" For a half second Drew wished he could visit with Nick and discover more about him. Not a good idea. Right now his rodeo schedule left little time for other commitments.

"Nick reads his storybooks before he turns out the light. He usually falls asleep around eight." She drained the water from the sink, then dried her hands on a clean towel and fixed herself a glass of tea. "Have a seat."

"Is he always so…" Drew struggled to find the right word when he joined Hallie at the table.

"Curious?"

He nodded.

"No more than any normal four-year-old," she said. "He's stubborn, too."

"Stubborn?"

"His feet have more suction power than a vacuum when his agenda differs from mine."

A surge of pride rushed through Drew. He'd been accused of stubbornness on occasion. He wondered how he could feel such an emotion when he didn't even *know* his son.

Hallie sipped her tea, then asked, "How are your ribs?"

That she cared surprised him—until he remembered she was a nurse. He suspected the question was as automatic as breathing to her. "The ribs are the least of my worries."

Her fingers tightened around the drinking glass, but that was the only clue she gave that his presence unnerved her.

"Tell me the truth. If I hadn't run into you earlier today at the hospital, would you have ever tracked me down and told me I had a son?"

"I don't know." Her next words cut him to the quick. "The last thing Nick needs in his life is a cowboy for a father."

What did Hallie see when she looked at him? A loser? A no-good rodeo bum? A man not good enough to be a father?

For the second time in his life Drew had fallen short. First, his own father, who'd believed Drew would never succeed at rodeo. Now Hallie, who for whatever reason believed cowboys weren't fit to be fathers.

Hell. Drew couldn't say for sure her impression of him was off the mark. The little boy sleeping down the hall deserved a committed father. Drew was committed, all right—but not to fatherhood.

"Why did you sleep with me?" The question shouted through his brain but escaped his mouth in a strangled whisper.

"Don't make more of that night than it was."

"And *what* exactly was that night to you?"

"Sex," she whispered. "We had sex, that's all."

Drew winced. Their one night of lovemaking hadn't been the least bit memorable for her. What had he expected—a gushing commentary on his male prowess? Embarrassed and angry, he lashed out. "Well, shoot, darlin'. Sorry I was a disappointment in the sack."

A pink tinge spread across her cheeks and one neatly trimmed fingernail tapped the table in a steady rhythm. That she wasn't as immune to him as she pretended to be took some of the sting out of her smackdown.

Curious about that night, he asked, "How did you get home?" He'd woken before dawn and discovered she'd left the camper. He'd been mad as hell and worried sick at the same time. The thought of her walking the streets alone had made him crazy. He'd driven all over Bastrop, searching for her, but she'd vanished into thin air.

"I called a friend and she picked me up at the campground." She sighed, the sound more telling than words.

Years of competing in the Bastrop rodeo looking for Hallie in the stands. Driving by the hospital hoping to catch a glimpse of her entering or leaving the building. He'd wasted hours…days…months…years thinking about her.

Hallie glanced at her watch. Her nerves had been tied in knots since Drew had entered the apartment. She had yet to figure out his agenda. The uncertainty of the situation made her queasy and anxious. "Say what you came to say then leave."

He removed a personal check from his shirt pocket. "This is for Nick."

Hallie's eyes fixated on the bank draft. Three thousand dollars.

"It's not much, considering—"

"I don't want your money." Hallie didn't want anything to do with Drew at all.

"Catching up on child support payments may take a while. Most of my cash is invested in the ranch. Once the rodeo season ends, I should be able to make monthly payments."

If Hallie accepted his money, Drew would assume he had rights where Nick was concerned. Those *rights* worried her. "Most men would demand proof a child was theirs."

Drew flashed a crooked grin and Hallie ignored the tingle in her stomach. The blasted cowboy was too handsome for his own good.

"Nick has my eyes and my chin. That's all the proof I need." His gaze pinned her. "You've given me no reason to trust you, but my gut says you wouldn't try to pass off another man's child as mine."

Drew's admission made Hallie feel guilty and grateful all at once. "Nick and I don't need your money. We're doing fine on our own." The sooner he understood she and Nick didn't need him, the better.

"I don't walk away from my responsibilities."

Darn his stubborn hide. "Why are you doing this?" Her eyes welled with tears and she prayed she wouldn't cry.

"I'm his father."

"You'll hurt him."

"Offering financial support will harm my son?"

"You're a cowboy."

"We're back to that again? If you object to cowboys why'd you leave Cozie's with me that night?"

Just like her mother, Hallie had fallen for a cowboy,

but this time she was determined her son wouldn't pay the price for his mother's bad judgment. "Nick will become attached to you, then one day he'll wake up and you'll be gone."

Drew stood so fast his chair crashed to the floor, startling them both. "Hold on now. Who said anything about me sticking around?"

Hallie's pulse quickened. Dare she hope? "Are you saying you don't want anything to do with Nick?"

"No. Yes."

Which is it?

He set the chair upright. "At the moment, child support is all I can manage."

Thank God. Relief—swift and sharp—swept through her. Drew noticed her reaction and frowned, but Hallie couldn't care less about sparing his feelings. "That's fine." If Drew had decided to stick around, it would only be a matter of time before Nick realized he wasn't a priority in Drew's life. Hallie had experienced that kind of neglect from her own father and wanted to spare her son the same pain.

"So we're good?" Drew asked.

Hallie heard the catch in his voice, but refused to make eye contact for fear she'd cave in to the cowboy and invite him to stop by and visit whenever an opportunity arose. She pushed the check across the table. "I won't take your money."

"It's not for you. It's for Nick."

They were at an impasse. Hallie didn't want Drew believing his money entitled him to a place in Nick's life. "It's too much."

"If you need extra cash my cell phone number is on

the check." He turned his back to her and walked out of the room.

A dull pain throbbed in her head as she followed him to the front door. Hand on the knob, Drew hesitated.

She waited. For a word. A gesture.

Anything that would prove he was different from her father.

"Lock up after me."

As soon as the door closed, Hallie sank onto the sofa and buried her face in her hands. Things had worked out for the best. Drew wanted nothing to do with her and Nick. She should be happy. Ecstatic. Relieved.

Instead, she felt like she'd failed her son.

"LADIES AND GENTLEMEN, turn your eyes to chute number four. Drew Rawlins of San Antonio is coming out on Strawberry Wine, a world famous bucker."

At the announcer's booming voice, Drew squeezed his legs against the gelding's quivering flanks and clutched the buck rein attached to the horse's halter until pain pulsed through the tendons in his gloved hand. The vest he wore to protect his healing ribs made drawing a deep breath impossible. Ready as he'd ever be, he slid low in the saddle, then nodded to the gate man.

The instant the horse cleared the chute the animal reared up and flailed his forelegs. Drew's thigh muscles clenched with the effort to hold tight to his seat while spurring the bronc from the points of its shoulders to the back of the saddle.

The gelding's front hooves hit the dirt. Hard.

The jarring impact rattled Drew's sore ribs, caused his back teeth to clamp together and damn near snapped his neck. Before he recovered, Strawberry Wine rocketed off the ground again and the arena lights bounced off the animal's belly.

Drew concentrated on establishing a scratching rhythm, but the gelding's wild gyrations made the kicking motion awkward. When he anticipated the horse twisting one way, the animal spun the other. Hell, this bronc was meaner and crazier than that son of a bitch Demon he'd ridden in Bastrop. In self-defense, Drew rotated his hand, coiling another inch of rope around the glove, and prayed the buzzer would go off.

Eight seconds wasn't an eternity, but when a cowboy straddled more than a thousand pounds of red rage, a second lasted a lifetime. As soon as the buzzer sounded above the roar of the crowd, a final surge of adrenaline shot through Drew's muscles. The ride wasn't over until his boots hit the dirt. Drew struggled to free his hand, but when the pickup men approached, the bronc bolted.

One cowboy used his horse to crowd Strawberry Wine against the rails, while the other moved in to help with the rein. Their worried expressions didn't bode well for Drew. If he couldn't free his hand, the bronc would tear his arm from the socket.

Drew worked two fingers beneath the rein, allowing the blood to flow to his fingers. Ignoring the prickling pain, he shifted in the saddle and rotated his shoulder.

Big mistake.

The bronc spun sideways. Caught off balance, Drew went flying. Instinctively, he turned. His shoulder slammed into the chute, taking the brunt of the impact. White-hot pain licked his tender ribs. Only the tips of his boots scraped the dirt as the beast dragged him across the arena.

Dark shadows crowded Drew's vision. He no longer felt his left hand, which worried him more than the fire blazing inside his chest. One of the pickup men shouted and Drew glanced up in time to see a shiny object arcing through the air. *Knife.*

The pickup men severed the buck rein from the halter and a moment later Drew collapsed in the dirt.

"Whoo-hee, buddy. That was a hell of a ride," the pickup man shouted before chasing the bronc out of the arena.

Praying he wouldn't puke in front of the fans, Drew got to his knees. His breath came in short, fiery gasps. The rope dangled from his wrist and there was no feeling left in his hand.

He stood. Stumbled once. Twice.

Slowly and steadily he shuffled toward the open gate twenty yards away. A hush settled over the crowd. Sheer male pride kept his legs from buckling beneath him.

When he reached the gate, Brody was there. "You all right, hoss?"

"Get me out of here." Drew leaned heavily against his friend.

Brody shoved his shoulder under Drew's armpit and dragged him into an empty stall. "Jeez, man. I thought you were a goner out there. What the hell happened?" Brody worked the rope and glove off Drew's injured hand. He whistled low between his teeth. "Doesn't look good. You ought to go to the first-aid station."

Already Drew's fingers had swollen to twice their normal size. If he couldn't grip the rope, he couldn't ride. He flexed his fingers, relieved when a sharp, stabbing pain attacked the joints. "What was my score?"

"Didn't you hear? Eighty-two. You beat Fitzgerald and Stover."

Relief rushed through Drew, replenishing his strength. After a disappointing month when he couldn't find his seat in the saddle, things were finally going his way. There was a good chance after today's competition he'd move into the top fifteen in the standings. "Has everyone ridden?"

"A couple of turds from the university gotta ride."

The arena buzzer sounded, and Brody poked his head out of the stall. "One turd down."

"Give me a minute, will you?"

"Sure." Brody hesitated outside the stall. "You haven't been the same, you know, since you found out about the boy."

Fear pulsed through Drew, and he locked his knees to keep from sliding to the ground. Brody was right. After running into Hallie a month ago in Bastrop, Drew's head had been so full of her and Nick that nothing else fit up there. He pressed his lips together—the only part of his body that didn't ache—and struggled to subdue the panic, which stung his gut like a swarm of wasps.

He should have been seriously injured today. The fact that he walked away from the ride with a badly bruised hand and a banged-up shoulder was a miracle. If he didn't straighten out his head before he rode again, he might as well write his will.

"Hoss?"

Hadn't Brody left? "What?"

"If you don't quit thinking about them, you won't win the title."

Drew listened to Brody's boot heels thud against the ground as he walked away. When he was positive his buddy wouldn't return, Drew collapsed to his knees in the straw. Alone, with no one to witness his disgrace, his body shook with fear.

Images of Hallie flooded his mind, and he focused on her blond hair, her pretty smile and big brown eyes. His thoughts drifted to the afternoon they'd met at the hospital five years ago and in a few minutes, his breathing calmed.

Hell. If things had gone a different way tonight…if he'd broken a rib and punctured a lung—or worse, his heart—he could have died on the arena floor in Hastings, Nebraska.

Died without ever having a relationship with his son. In the furthest corner of his heart, Drew had tucked away his feelings for Hallie, believing nothing would ever come of them. Now she was back in his life in a way he'd never imagined and he wondered if he could find the strength to forgive her.

He sat in the stall sorting through his thoughts long after the bronc-riding competition had ended and he'd been declared the winner. Everything made sense now. Drew knew what he had to do—claim his rightful place in his son's life.

Chapter Four

Drew stood outside Hallie's apartment Saturday night, doubts about his latest revelation sucking the courage out of him. Even now he wasn't sure if he'd returned to Bastrop to appease his conscience or because he truly wanted a relationship with his son. He worried about Hallie's reaction to his decision to become more involved in Nick's life. Would she reject his good intentions or praise him for trying to do the right thing?

Does it matter what she thinks? Yes. No. Hell, he didn't know.

Suddenly the apartment door opened and he came face-to-face with Nick and *Aunt Sharon.*

"I know you," Nick said.

"Hi there, buddy." Drew grinned at the boy, then held his hand out to the woman. "Hello, Aunt Sharon. I'm—"

"Drew Rawlins." Green eyes perused him from head-to-toe. "How are your ribs?"

"Ribs are fine." They'd be less sore if he'd give his bones a chance to rest, but with the finals in three months he couldn't afford to cut any rodeos from his schedule.

"He's a real cowboy, Aunt Sharon."

Nick's smile triggered an achy, tight feeling in Drew's chest.

"I heard," Aunt Sharon said.

"You bust broncs, right, mister?"

"That's right." Drew never wanted his son to lose that sparkle of awe in his eyes when he spoke of his father.

"Aunt Sharon's gonna take me for ice cream. Wanna come?"

Drew had been hoping to get back on the road before dark. He glanced at Sharon. "Is Hallie home?"

"She's on a date."

A sharp twinge poked Drew's side—probably one of his bruised ribs acting up.

"You're welcome to join us for ice cream." Sharon took Nick's hand and stepped outside the apartment, then locked the door.

"We're going to the Freeze Top," Nick said.

"It's a couple of blocks away." Sharon started down the sidewalk with Nick.

Drew would tag along because he wanted to spend time with his son, not because he hoped to find out more about Hallie's date.

Nick raced off and Sharon called after him. "Don't get too far ahead." The boy changed course and chased a squirrel up a tree.

"He's stubborn." Sharon glanced at Drew. "Maybe he inherited that trait from his father."

"Hallie told you?"

Sharon nodded. "I imagine you're upset that she kept Nick a secret from you."

Taken back by the blunt assessment Drew mumbled,

"A little." More than a *little,* but that was between him and Hallie.

"You should be *a lot* mad." They walked in silence to the corner. "Hands, Nick." The boy reached for his aunt's hand, then surprised Drew by grabbing his. The small fingers in Drew's grip felt odd yet comfortable at the same time.

After they crossed the street, Nick skipped ahead. Before Drew lost his nerve, he asked, "Who's the guy Hallie's out with tonight?"

Sharon's eyes twinkled.

"I'm not jealous," Drew insisted. "I just want to make sure he's a decent man if he's going to be around my son."

"You know him," Sharon said. "He's the doctor who checked you over in the E.R."

Mark Feller. What did Hallie see in the arrogant jerk? "Have they dated long?"

"No. Mark's new to the area. He's been after Hallie to go out on a second date and tonight she finally agreed."

Two dates hardly made them a couple.

"Thinking about giving the doctor a little competition?"

Drew's face warmed. "I don't have time for personal relationships." Trying to establish one with Nick would be difficult enough, let alone adding Hallie into the mix.

"It's amazing what people make time for if they really care to." Sharon pointed ahead. "Here we are."

Drew held open the door of the Freeze Top ice cream

shop, then followed Sharon and Nick inside. The place was packed.

A woman busing a table across the room gave Sharon a thumbs-up sign when she spotted Drew. Sharon laughed. "Don't worry. No one believes I'd date a guy like you."

"Why not?" he asked.

"Because I prefer brains over looks."

"Ouch."

"You quit rodeoing and let the other half of your brain grow back and I might be interested."

"I know a few cowboys who are into red hair. I could introduce you to one of them."

"Don't tempt me. I'm getting up there in years. Before long I may be desperate enough to date a cowboy."

A teenager behind the counter greeted them. "Hi, Nick."

"Hi, Emily." Nick turned to Drew. "She babysits me sometimes."

Emily batted her eyelashes. "Who's your friend, Nick?"

"He's my mom's cowboy."

Uh-oh.

"Wow. Your mom's a lucky lady. Wish I had a cowboy."

Drew ignored Sharon's strangled laughter. "I'm Hallie's—" He'd been about to say *friend*, but he and Hallie were hardly friends. "I'm an acquaintance of Hallie's."

Emily popped her gum. "Same flavor, Nick?"

"Yep. Root beer."

Drew dug out his wallet and motioned for Sharon to

put her purse away. After she requested strawberry, he added a black cherry cone to the order.

"There's seating outside." Sharon led them to a patio with umbrella tables. She waved to several people who called out hellos to her and Nick.

"How long have you lived in Bastrop?" Drew asked once they were seated.

"All my life. My folks have been gone for years, but I have a brother who lives with his family in Austin and a sister who lives in Dallas."

He guessed Sharon's age to be around forty. She caught him staring at her bare ring finger. "A long time ago I was engaged, then my fiancé decided he didn't want to live in Bastrop. I refused to leave, so we parted ways." Sharon licked the ice cream dripping down the side of her cone. "Where are you from?"

"I grew up in Bulverde."

"I've heard of the place."

"My grandfather owned a corner market there. My father ran the store until he died then my mother sold the property and moved in with her sister in Hollywood Park, north of San Antonio. When I'm not rodeoing, I hang my hat at a small ranch outside Lakerville."

"How come you're not busting broncs, mister?" Nick's mouth was smeared with ice cream.

"Well, I—"

"Nick, run inside and fetch some napkins for us." As soon as Nick obeyed, Sharon said, "Hallie is like a sister to me. I supported her through her pregnancy when you weren't there."

"I wasn't there because I didn't know." Even though he remained angry at Hallie for cheating him out of that experience with her, he was grateful she'd had a friend to lean on after she'd become pregnant.

"Hallie's done a heck of a job being both mother and father to Nick as well as providing him with a decent home and a life filled with friends and people who care about him. I'll never forgive you if you destroy what she's worked so hard to build."

"I'm not here to cause Hallie grief." *I'm here because of my son.*

"See that it stays that way."

Nick returned with a handful of napkins. "Emily says you're cute."

"Nope. Emily thinks you're cute," Drew teased.

Nick giggled. "Girls are gross. Right, Aunt Sharon?"

"Oh, yeah, we're really gross." Sharon tweaked Nick's nose.

"Do you like sports, Nick?" Drew was surprised at how easy it was to talk to his son.

"My friend Benny and I play soccer at school."

"What school do you go to?"

"Red Robin."

"Red Robin is a day care and preschool all in one," Sharon explained.

"Benny and I ride the bus to the Red Robin." Nick raised his arms above his head. "There's a big bird on the top of the bus."

Once Nick finished his ice cream, Sharon announced it was time to head home. Drew was reluctant to leave. He'd enjoyed chatting with Nick and found the boy entertaining and a lot less scary than he'd imagined.

When they arrived at the apartment, Sharon said, "Nick, go inside and get your overnight bag."

"See ya, mister." Nick waved to Drew, then entered the apartment.

Sharon's big-boned frame blocked the doorway. "Nick's spending the night at my house, in case..." She smiled.

In case Hallie decided to invite Dr. Feller in for a nightcap. "If Hallie checks in with you later tonight, tell her I'll be by in the morning before I head out of town." Looked as if he'd have to park his camper somewhere and wait until tomorrow to speak with Hallie.

"Will do. 'Night." The door shut in his face.

Drew drove to the campground he'd stayed at during the Bastrop Rodeo. They were full up. He returned to Hallie's apartment complex and parked in the shadows at the back of the lot beneath a cluster of overgrown trees. Hopefully no one—Miss Rose in particular—would notice the camper and call the police.

The clock said ten-thirty. Exhausted, he stretched out on the bed above the front seats. He wished he had someone to talk to, but Brody didn't carry a cell phone and until Drew figured out where he stood with Hallie and Nick, he didn't want to tell his mother she had a grandson. No sense getting her excited for nothing if Hallie refused to allow Nick to meet Drew's mother.

Left alone with his thoughts, Drew closed his eyes. He might as well catch a few winks while he could. Sleep would become a luxury if Hallie agreed to his plan to visit Nick between rodeos.

The sound of squealing tires woke Drew a short time later. He stumbled from the bunk and peered out the window at the back of the camper. A fancy sports car pulled up in front of Hallie's apartment. Wild horses couldn't have pulled Drew away from the window. A minute passed, then another and another, and Drew wondered what the two were doing behind the dark-tinted windows.

Kissing. Drew shook his head to erase the image of Hallie and the doctor in a heated embrace. Her personal life wasn't any of his business. Time crawled by before the passenger-side door opened and Hallie stepped from the car. A second later Feller drove off.

THE WIND KICKED UP and Hallie breathed in rain-scented air. The second weekend of September had ushered in a string of thunderstorms. Typical early fall weather in Texas—blistering hot one day, wet and cool the next. She stood in the parking lot, watching her date drive away. The sound of burning rubber echoed through the night when Mark turned onto the main road and sped away. She didn't blame him—not after she'd confessed friendship was all she had to offer him.

Mark shouldn't have been surprised—she'd been dis-tracted all night by thoughts of Drew. She should have never agreed to a second date with Mark, but she hadn't been able to get Drew off her mind. She'd hoped Mark would make her forget the cowboy, but the date had backfired. She'd spent the evening comparing Mark to Drew. The doctor hadn't stood a chance against the cow-boy's good looks and sexy charm. Hallie strolled along the sidewalk leading to her apartment, but switched di-rections when she noticed an unfamiliar vehicle parked at the back of the lot next to the Dumpster. She gaped at the camper. Drew Rawlins was back in town, which meant only one thing—trouble. The rear door swung open.

"What are you doing here?" She winced at the sound of her waspish voice.

Drew walked toward her. When he was within spitting distance, he whispered, "Keep your voice down or you'll wake Miss Rose."

Hallie shivered as he stood close enough that the scent of his aftershave mixed with the muggy air made her head spin.

"Feller's an ass."

She gasped.

"He didn't even walk you to the door."

Her heart sighed. Darn Drew and his cowboy chivalry. It would be so easy to fall for the man a second time.

"Aren't you supposed to be in Nebraska?" Now that Hallie had a moment to collect her senses, she noticed the haggard lines around his mouth and eyes. Drew was worn out.

"Nebraska was last weekend. I competed today in the San Patricio Pro Rodeo in Abilene."

Abilene was four and half hours away. Good grief. Drew should have rested tonight instead of driving two hundred and fifty miles to reach Bastrop. *He's not yours to worry about, Hallie.*

"Invite me in. We need to talk."

Hallie hesitated. "Not tonight, Drew. Nick's staying with a friend and—"

"Sharon answered the door when I got here earlier

this evening. We took Nick out for ice cream, then they left for her place."

The sooner Drew had his say, the sooner he'd leave. She led the way back to her apartment, but before she'd inserted the key, the door next to her opened.

"Hallie? Everything all right, dear?"

"Hello, Miss Rose. Everything's fine."

"Why, it's you again." Miss Rose stepped onto the sidewalk. "Is this cowboy bothering you?"

"This is Drew Rawlins." Hallie choked on her next words. "He's an old friend."

Drew tipped his hat. "Evenin', Miss Rose."

"Awful late for a social call." The elderly woman glanced at Hallie. "You have my number, dear, if you need me." She scowled at Drew, before shutting her door.

Drew followed Hallie into her apartment, then secured the locks. "Does the woman ever sleep?"

"Not really. But it's nice having her look out for me." Hallie didn't have a mother or grandmother and appreciated Miss Rose's concern.

"Hallie, I..." Drew's voice trailed off when his eyes landed on her cocktail dress—more specifically the cleavage exposed by the plunging neckline.

"Be right back." She marched to her bedroom, threw on the rattiest pair of sweats and ugliest T-shirt she owned, then returned to the living room. Drew exhaled loudly and she wondered if he'd held his breath the entire time she'd been gone—served the insensitive lug right for dropping by uninvited.

Against her better judgment she asked, "Coffee?"

His shoulders drooped. "Coffee would be good."

Hallie opened her mouth to ask if he'd won in Abilene, but changed her mind. Sundays were the final day of competition at most rodeos. Drew showing up at the apartment on a Saturday night meant he hadn't ridden well enough to make the final day.

She prepared a pot of coffee, then filled two mugs and brought them to the table, where she noticed Drew's swollen hand. Faded black-and-blue welts crisscrossed the knuckles. She probed the injury, ignoring the electric charge zapping her fingertips. "How did this happen?"

"Got tangled in the buck rein."

Resisting the urge to caress the swollen knuckles, she turned his hand over and examined his callused palm. "You should sit out a few rodeos."

"Looks worse than it is." He tugged free of her grasp.

She thought of all the times she'd bandaged Nick's cuts and scrapes and offered kisses to ease the pain. Who did Drew turn to for sympathy? *Don't ask.* Ignoring his protest, she grabbed two ice packs from the freezer and set his palm on top of one and laid the other across his knuckles.

"Hallie." The ominous tone in his voice gave her pause. "I've given this a lot of thought.…"

Fearing she knew what he intended to say, Hallie snatched the dishrag from the sink and wiped off the already clean countertop.

"I want to be involved in my son's life. Nick needs to know who his father is."

She clenched the rag until her thumbnail tore through

the cotton. Panic clawed its way up her throat, and she swallowed hard.

"Hallie…?"

She wanted what was best for her son, but feared Drew's good intentions would end in disaster, leaving her to pick up the pieces of Nick's broken heart.

And what about her? Would Nick push her aside to make room for Drew? "Why the sudden change of heart?"

"My son needs a man in his life."

"Nick has men he can—"

"The moron who left you standing alone in the parking lot isn't fit to be your lover let alone a male role model for my son."

And Drew believed he was better? "You don't know anything about my relationship with Mark."

"I know there is no relationship."

Embarrassed that he'd picked up on the truth, she snapped, "Oh, really?"

"Darlin', if you'd worn that skimpy dress for me, there's no way in hell I'd drop you off at the curb and drive away."

"What would you do?" The question slipped from her mouth in a breathless whisper.

His blue eyes darkened to indigo. "I'd be all over you like dust on a cowboy after a long day in the saddle."

Before the conversation turned down the wrong path—one that led to more regrets—she asked, "What do you mean by involved in Nick's life?"

"I'll stop by for a visit when I'm passing through town and I'll call Nick as often as possible."

An hour here or there. Hallie knew from experience

a few hours every once in a great while was worse than never seeing a parent. "Sounds like you'd rather be an uncle instead of a father."

Drew swirled the coffee in his mug. "It's the best I can do right now with my schedule." He cleared his throat. "You have my word that I'll do right by Nick."

Panic filled her lungs until they pinched. "Your word isn't good enough."

"After keeping my son a secret from me, my word is more than you deserve." He expelled a rough breath, then winced.

"Your ribs are bothering you." Drew pushed himself too hard.

"Forget my ribs." His next words cut her to the quick. "You've had Nick all to yourself for four years. I want my share of time with him."

"What happens when you leave?" she asked.

"What are you talking about?"

"What happens to Nick, when you've had your fill of playing *Daddy,* and you no longer want the responsibility?"

He shoved his chair away from the table and paced across the room. Instead of answering her question, he said, "Don't make this harder than it has to be. I have legal rights."

"One child-support payment doesn't guarantee you any rights."

"If I have to, I'll take you to court."

The threat slammed into Hallie. "You don't have time for a custody battle." She certainly didn't have the money for one. She was still paying back student loans for her nursing degree.

"A lawyer can handle things while I'm on the road," he said.

"Cowboys make terrible fathers." She ought to know—her father had ridden bulls, until one had ended his life.

"For a woman who doesn't think highly of cowboys, I'd sure as hell like to know why you slept with me."

Refusing to allow Drew to change the subject, she said, "You know nothing about being a father."

"What difference does that make? I have to try. I owe Nick at least that much."

"Even if you end up hurting him?" *Hurting me?* Hallie cursed the tears that flooded her eyes.

"I won't hurt Nick."

She'd never felt such a lack of control over the future, not even when she'd been pregnant and alone. Yes, Nick deserved a chance to be with his father, but she couldn't trust Drew not to break their son's heart. And the thought of Drew threatening the close relationship she had with Nick scared Hallie. Right now she was her son's whole world. Would Nick feel the same way about her once he heard Drew was his father? She knew she couldn't compete with an exciting bronc buster in her son's eyes.

Drew leaned over the table. "I'll be in El Paso next weekend. I'll stop by after the rodeo and we'll tell Nick then."

"But—" He pressed a finger against her lips and his cool breath fanned her cheek. The subtlety of his stare was powerful. Dangerous. His gaze lulled her into complacency, weakened her resolve to resist her attraction to him.

"Don't try to stop me from seeing my son. The fact that you didn't tell me you were pregnant with Nick all those years ago cancels your say in my relationship with Nick. Whether you like it or not I'm going to get to know my son. And I—not you—will set the ground rules."

Speechless, Hallie watched Drew walk out of the kitchen. A moment later the slamming of the front door shattered her composure and the tears she'd held at bay for weeks poured from her eyes.

DREW DRAINED THE BEER bottle in four swallows, then set it on the bar with a thunk. The barkeep looked his way, but Drew waved him off. His favorite cold brew suddenly tasted stale. The door opened and in sauntered a group of Hell's Angels, in full leather regalia, as they swaggered up to the bar.

The beer joint was like every other Drew had visited on the road—loud music and the stink of sweaty bodies. He studied the bottles of inspiration lined three rows deep behind the bartender. An hour had passed since he'd left Hallie's apartment. He should be halfway to his ranch, but fear had kept him from driving beyond the outskirts of Bastrop.

Fear. Fear he wouldn't be able to live up to his son's expectations. Short of giving up rodeo, Drew intended to bust his ass to be part of Nick's life—he owed the boy at least that much. Nick was his son and even if Drew couldn't be with him on a day-to-day basis, he wanted the boy to know he mattered to his father.

But would his best effort be good enough?

Two and a half months and a handful of rodeos stood

between him and the NFR in December. Drew ignored the voice in his head that insisted Nick and Hallie would interfere with his quest for the title. After he won, Drew would have all the time in the world to focus on his son. For now, he had to find a way to juggle fatherhood and rodeo. One thing was for sure, he'd never be able to concentrate on bustin' broncs until he'd squared things with Nick.

He tossed an Abe Lincoln on the bar, then left the tavern. He admired Hallie's fierce determination to protect their son, but if Drew intended to establish a relationship with Nick he needed Hallie's support. He stepped away from the entrance and retrieved his cell phone from his pocket. Hallie answered on the fourth ring.

"Hello?"

Hallie's sleep-drugged voice conjured up an image of her naked body stretching beneath cool cotton sheets. "It's me."

"Drew? What happened?"

"Nothing. Sorry, I woke you."

"It's okay. I just crawled into bed."

Shoving a hand through his hair, he leaned against the building and closed his eyes. "I want this situation with Nick straightened out before I leave town." Silence greeted his statement. "You there?"

"What happened to waiting until after the rodeo in El Paso?"

"You planning to run from this like you ran from me that night in my camper?"

"How dare—"

"I dare, Hallie." He kicked the plastic garbage can

chained to the downspout against the side of the building. "Nick's gone four years without knowing his father. I don't want to make him wait another day."

"Okay. You win."

Hallie's surrender didn't make Drew feel any better. "I'll take you and Nick out for supper tomorrow. Let Nick choose the restaurant."

"Fine." Hallie's voice wobbled and he worried she'd burst into tears.

He wished he could reassure her that everything would be okay. But honest to God, he didn't know if any of them would emerge from their situation unchanged or unharmed. "Everything'll work out, Hallie."

"Drew…"

"What?"

"Be careful how you tell Nick about our encounter five years ago."

Encounter? They'd gone from making love, to just sex, to an encounter—Hallie was hell on his ego. "I promise." He disconnected the call, wondering how many promises he'd have to make in order to carve out a place for himself in Nick's life.

Chapter Five

Late Sunday afternoon Drew knocked on Hallie's apartment door. He was both nervous and excited about telling Nick he was his father. He'd spent the day rehearsing speeches in his head, but none of them had felt right. In the end, Drew had decided he'd wing it with Nick and hope he didn't sound like a blundering idiot.

The door opened and Drew smiled. "Hey, sport. How are you?"

"Mom says you're gonna take us out for pizza."

"That's right, I—" Feminine laughter followed by a baritone chuckle echoed from somewhere in the apartment. Who was Hallie entertaining? "Where's your mom?"

"In the kitchen."

Drew stepped inside, then shut the door behind him. "Who else is in the kitchen?"

"Dr. Feller. He brought Mom flowers." Nick pointed to the vase on the coffee table.

Roses? A sharp pang shot through Drew, but he denied it was jealousy.

Hallie was a mature, single woman. She could date who she wanted to. *Even jerks.*

"Wanna see the new Hot Wheels car Dr. Feller gave me?" Nick dropped to his knees on the carpet, shoved his hand beneath the couch, then produced a shiny red sports car. "He said it's just like his car."

Drew would have offered to buy a Hot Wheels camper but doubted Nick would find the model as exciting as a sports car. While Nick drove the toy car across the coffee table, Drew strolled through the room and paused in the kitchen doorway. Hallie and Feller were sitting at the table chatting over glasses of iced tea.

"Hate to interrupt, but I believe we have a dinner date," Drew said.

Hallie jumped up from her chair, but Feller remained seated, a wide grin on his face.

"Mark, you remember Drew Rawlins, don't you?" Hallie glanced between the two men.

Mark's gaze assessed Drew. "The cowboy with the bruised ribs."

"Ribs are fine now," Drew said, hoping to discourage the doctor from asking a bunch of medical questions.

Feller winked at Hallie. "Think about the zoo and let me know later."

"I will. Thanks for stopping by."

Drew stepped aside, allowing Feller to pass through the doorway. Hallie made no move to walk the doctor to the door, which pleased Drew.

"Have fun eating pizza, Nick," Feller said on his way out.

Drew struggled to control his jealousy. He had no claim on Hallie and didn't understand why he cared one way or another whom she dated. *You care because she's the mother of your son.* That made sense. Now if only he could buy in to the logic. "Are you serious about Feller?"

Hallie fidgeted with the buttons on her blouse. "We're friends."

"He brought you roses." *And gave my son a present.*

"The flowers were an apology."

"For what?"

"For—" Hallie waved a hand in the air. "Never mind. Mark and I talked things out and decided we were better off being friends."

"Is that why he invited you and Nick to the zoo?"

"Yes."

"Are you going?"

"Probably. Nick loves the zoo and we haven't been to San Antonio in a while."

Drew was Nick's father. He should be the one taking his son to the zoo. *You don't have time.* He'd make time. *When?* He was on the road from now until Thanksgiving.

Speaking of the road... "We'd better get going." He walked into the living room. "Have you picked a place to eat, Nick?"

"Yeah. I wanna go to Buck's."

"Buck's it is then." Buck's might not be as exciting as the zoo, but it was the best Drew could do under the circumstances.

WHEN NICK PICKED Buck's Pizza for dinner Drew hadn't thought anything of it, until they stepped inside. The place was packed. Several patrons stared at him—a reminder that he was on Hallie's home turf.

The strong smell of bread dough and Italian seasonings made Drew nauseous—or was it the fear Nick would reject him as a father that tied his gut in knots?

"Hallie!" A woman in the dining area stood at her table and waved.

"That's Denise. She's a nurse at the hospital," Hallie said.

Drew should have suggested the hot dog stand near the bar he'd drank at last night. No one would have eavesdropped on them out on the highway.

"Look, Mom, there's Matt." Nick pointed to a boy sitting in a booth with an elderly couple.

"Kinda crowded in here," Drew said, hoping Hallie would suggest another restaurant.

"Leaving now will cause more gossip." Hallie smiled at the hostess when she approached. "Table for three, please."

"Right this way." The teen led them to the back corner of the dining room—at least they'd have privacy.

Drew held out a chair for Hallie and couldn't help admiring the way her loose hair fell over her shoulders in big fat curls. He curbed his desire to touch the silky strands and scolded himself for becoming sidetracked when Nick deserved his undivided attention tonight.

"Can I go see Matt?" Nick asked.

"Sure." Once Nick bolted, Hallie said, "I've lived in Bastrop most of my life. Working at the hospital, living in an apartment complex and having a son in preschool brings me in contact with a lot of the locals."

Shoot, Drew met his share of people on the road, but he never remained in one place long enough to establish lifelong friendships. He knew a slew of cowboys on the circuit, but they weren't friends, they were competitors—except for Brody.

"Hey, Hallie." A tall, dark-haired woman placed three glasses of water on the table.

"Hi, Claire." When the woman stared at Drew, Hallie said, "Claire, I'd like you to meet Drew Rawlins. Drew, this is my neighbor, Claire Bailey. Her son Robert goes to the same day care as Nick."

"Nice to meet you, Claire."

"Likewise." Claire smacked her gum. "You look familiar."

"Drew competed in the Homecoming Rodeo." Hallie glanced at Drew. "Claire's a big fan of cowboys."

Meaning Hallie wasn't?

The waitress snapped her fingers. "You're that bronc rider who fell off his horse and had to be taken to the hospital by ambulance."

"I got bucked off."

"Uh-huh. You get hurt bad?"

Didn't the woman have other customers to wait on? "I'm fine, thanks for asking."

"We'd like to order a large pepperoni pizza. I'll take a Diet Coke and Nick will have a root beer."

"I'll have a root beer, too," Drew said. "And could you add sausage on half that pizza?"

"Sure thing." Claire collected the menus and departed.

"You said you lived here most of your life. Where were you born?" Drew asked.

"Eleven miles west of Bastrop in unincorporated Cedar Creek."

"Was your father a farmer?"

Hallie stared unseeingly across the table as if caught up in a memory from the past. Then she blinked. "My father wasn't in the picture much and my mother bartended. We lived in a trailer behind the bar."

The childhood picture Hallie painted wasn't pretty. "How did you end up in Bastrop?"

"My mother died when I was seven and I was placed in a foster home here in town." For the first time since they'd begun discussing her family, Hallie's expression lightened. "My foster mother, Margaret O'Fallen, was a middle-aged widow without any children of her own. She officially adopted me when I turned twelve." The sparkle in Hallie's eyes dimmed. "She died before Nick was born. She would have loved being a grandmother."

"I bet she's looking down on you and smiling," Drew said, even though he wasn't sure he believed dead people could watch over their loved ones on earth. If the deceased could, then his father probably cheered against him each time Drew climbed on the back of a bronc.

"Sorry that took so long." Claire returned with their drinks. She grinned at Drew. "Joe says you're pretty good at bustin' broncs."

"Who's Joe?" Drew asked.

"Kid who works in the kitchen. You could give him some pointers. He's been thinking about trying his hand at rodeo."

Real cowboys didn't *try* rodeo—it wasn't a sport you flirted with. Rodeo was dangerous and deadly and any cowboy who thought it was easy was smokin' dope. Just ask Brody.

"How long before the pizza, Claire?"

"Fifteen minutes. Why?" Claire frowned. "You in a hurry?"

"Yes," Drew said.

"No," Hallie said.

Claire arched an eyebrow. "Okay then." She walked off.

Nick returned to the table and slid onto his chair. He sucked down half his root beer before gasping for air. "Matt's dad's a policeman. He showed me and Matt his gun and told us guns are bad and we're not supposed to ever touch one."

"Good advice. Guns aren't toys," Drew said.

"Yeah, Matt's lucky 'cause his dad's got a cool job."

What would Nick think about Drew's job? The past few weeks, Drew had repeated the word *dad* over and over in his mind. The title felt funny—not bad. Just... different.

"Pizza's here," Claire called out a little while later as she approached the table. "Can I get you anything else?"

"No, thanks. This looks great," Hallie said.

Nick bit off a big chunk of pizza. "Slow down, buddy." The boy's grin spawned a warm sensation in Drew's chest.

They ate in silence for several minutes, then Hallie pushed her chair back and stood. "I'm going to the ladies room."

Left alone with Nick, Drew was at a loss for words. Nick finished his pizza, then made engine sounds as he drove the salt-and-pepper shakers around the table.

"Rrrrumm." His cheeks puffed and spit flew from his mouth.

Drew remembered buying a dirt bike at a yard sale when he'd turned fifteen. He'd spent the summer tinkering with the motor, then totaled it his first time out. From that day forward, he'd parked his backside on horses.

"Do you and your mom come here often?" Drew asked.

"No, 'cause Mom says we gotta save money for my college." Nick frowned. "What's a college?"

"A big school."

"Bigger than Red Robin?"

"Yep. College is a lot bigger."

"Oh."

While Nick drove the shakers around the table, guilt gnawed at Drew's gut. Hallie was sacrificing to raise their son and plan for his future. Once Drew finished the rodeo season he needed to set up a fund to help Hallie pay for Nick's college and anything else his son required as he grew up.

"Can I go play?" Nick nodded to the arcade at the back of the dining room.

Drew wasn't sure if Hallie had a rule about finishing his meal before playing, but Nick was wound up and needed a break from eating. "Sure. Only one game, then we'll eat another slice of pizza." Ignoring the stares that followed them, Drew clasped Nick's hand and walked him to the arcade. As soon as they entered the room, Nick raced from one video game to the next, pushing all the buttons.

"Let's play basketball," Drew said. They took turns

shooting until the buzzer sounded. Nick made two baskets, Drew twelve.

"You're good." Nick's praise made Drew feel like a Wheaties box sports hero.

"I always wanted to try out for the basketball team in high school," Drew said.

"You did?"

"Yep, but I had to work in my grandpa's grocery store."

"That sucks."

"Nicholas Drew," a feminine voice called. Hallie stood a few feet away.

Nicholas Drew? She'd given their son Drew's name. *Why?* The possibility she cared about him more than she let on sent Drew's heart tripping over itself. The feeling didn't last. If he'd meant anything at all to Hallie, she wouldn't have kept Nick a secret.

"I'm not supposed to say that word," Nick whispered.

Drew grinned. "Stinks. Nick said 'that stinks.'"

Hallie's lips twitched, but her eyes remained solemn. "I thought that's what you said, young man." She caressed Nick's cheek.

Drew was envious of Hallie and Nick's relationship, but knowing she loved the boy—a part of Drew—so fiercely and completely, eased some of the loneliness inside him.

"Can we play a video game now?" Nick pleaded.

"You know the rule, honey. Go finish your supper."

"Sorry," Drew said. "That's my fault. I thought it would be okay if he played a game until you returned to the table."

Hallie watched Nick cut through the dining area. "You have to keep your guard up around him. He'll push the boundaries every time, if he believes he can get away with it."

They joined Nick at the table and Hallie served everyone a second slice of pizza. *Now or never.* Drew pushed his plate aside and straightened his spine. He didn't know the first thing about talking to a kid. Shoot, the last child he'd exchanged more than a few words with was a rodeo clown's son at the Calgary Stampede—a year ago.

"Nick, I need to tell you—"

"Happy birthday, Sue!" A chorus of voices singing the birthday song interrupted Drew. A waitress presented a slice of apple pie to the birthday girl.

While Nick watched the celebration, Drew noticed Hallie's worried expression. Her expectations of him as a father were pretty steep. He'd be a liar if he claimed he could meet them. He hated to disappoint her, but he didn't have a whole lot of confidence that he wouldn't.

After a troubled relationship with his own father, Drew yearned to connect with Nick on a deeper level. But in the long run, Drew feared he'd disappoint them all. For a split second he thought of walking away— for Nick's sake. Then Nick tugged his shirtsleeve and said, "I like apple pie," and suddenly leaving wasn't an option. No matter the outcome tonight Drew was in the fatherhood business for the long haul.

"I..." Drew hesitated.

Hallie flashed a shaky smile but offered no reassuring words.

There were few experiences in Drew's life that he

could count on remembering forever.… His first rodeo ride. His father's death. The night in his camper with Hallie. The afternoon he'd met Nick for the first time. And here was number five on his list of forever memories.… "I'm your father, Nick."

Nothing. Just a blank stare.

"Honey?" Hallie touched Nick's arm.

The boy ignored his mother, his eyes narrowing on Drew. "How come you didn't never wanna see me?"

The agony was swift and sharp in Drew's chest, as if he'd been punched with a red-hot branding iron. Up to now the boy's life had been a lie. His son deserved the truth, but Drew didn't have the heart to tell Nick that his mother had intentionally deceived both of them. "Your mom and I knew each other briefly. Then I went away for a long time."

"Were you dead?"

He opened his mouth to speak, but the words stuck to the sides of his throat.

"No, sweetheart, your father wasn't dead." Hallie's tortured expression pleaded with Drew.

"I stayed away, buddy, because of my job."

"You mean 'cause you ride broncs?"

"That's right. I travel all over the country competing in rodeos. I never stay in one place for very long. And I didn't have a home of my own until I bought my ranch a year ago."

"But didn't you wanna come see me sometimes?" Nick whispered.

Drew's lungs cinched together, making breathing impossible. Gazing into his son's blameless eyes, so like his own, he silently cursed Hallie. *I'm not the bad guy, damn it.*

"If your father had known about you, he would have stopped by to visit," Hallie said.

"Your mom's right. I would have come back long ago."

Nick's forehead scrunched. He looked at Hallie. "How come you couldn't find my dad?"

Because she chose not to. Drew clenched his jaw until the bone threatened to crack. The past couple of minutes, his son's life had been turned upside down. Although Drew wanted to blame Hallie, he wouldn't threaten the one sure thing in Nick's life—his mother.

Hallie's chin trembled, but Drew kept his eyes trained on Nick. "Your mom tried, but she couldn't find me." His stomach convulsed around the lie.

"But we coulda waited at your ranch. Right, Mom?"

God help him, Drew was in over his head.

"I didn't know about the ranch," Hallie said.

"How come you came back now?" Nick mumbled.

This wasn't fair. He shouldn't have to defend himself to his own son. "Remember when we bumped into each other at the hospital?"

Nick refused to look at Drew.

"That's when I found out you were my son."

The boy remained silent so long, Drew began to worry. Hallie was no help. She stared into space, her face pale, her eyes haunted.

"It'll take some time to get used to the idea of having a dad. But I want you to know—" when Drew paused, Nick glanced up "—that I'm real proud to have you as my son." He rubbed Nick's back. "I think I even like you better than those ornery old broncs I ride." His joke fell flat as Nick sat stone-faced.

Hallie wanted to cry. For Nick. For herself. Even for Drew. The moment Nick had been told Drew was his father, her son's relationship with her had changed. *Forever.*

There was no longer a need for Hallie to be both mother and father. In truth, she was relieved to have some of the parenting responsibility lifted from her shoulders, but at the same time she resented not having full control of Nick. She vowed she'd do everything in her power to make sure her son never regretted having Drew for a father.

"Can I tell my friends I got a dad?"

"You can tell anyone you want," Drew said.

Nick's expression lightened, easing Hallie's anxiety.

"I wanna go shoot more baskets," Nick said.

"You—"

"Go ahead," Drew interrupted and fished fifty cents from his pocket. "I'll be right there."

Taking a deep breath, Hallie composed herself. She'd always made the decisions where Nick was concerned and she didn't like Drew assuming that role. The idea of her son seeking Drew's permission for anything didn't sit well with her.

As soon as Nick left the table, Drew said, "He took the news well."

Maybe. But what about tomorrow? Or a week from now when the reality of having an absentee father sank in? "It's a little early to know how this will affect him."

"What's the matter?" Drew's mouth pressed into a thin line. "Did I screw up?"

"No." He'd painted himself the villain and made Hallie appear innocent. "Thank you for not telling Nick that I could have tracked you down." When her son was older, he'd learn the truth—that even though it was wrong she'd wanted to spare him from experiencing what she'd gone through with her own father.

"But you didn't want to find me, did you?" Drew toyed with his fork. "When the time is right, I'll make sure Nick hears my side of the story."

The blood rushed from Hallie's face, leaving her light-headed. What if Drew planned to earn Nick's love and trust, then challenge her for guardianship? "Please don't use Nick to get back at me."

Drew tossed his napkin on the table and walked away.

Hallie doubted Nick would ever experience a normal father-son relationship with Drew and after today, it was anybody's guess when Nick would see his father again.

Fifteen minutes later father and son returned to the table. "Ready to leave?" Drew asked.

More than ready.

Nick's incessant chatter made the drive to the apartment blessedly short. Drew walked them to the door.

Before she had a chance to thank him for meal, Nick tugged Drew's pant leg. "What are we gonna do tomorrow?"

"Honey, your dad has to leave town."

"Oh." Nick scuffed the toe of his shoe against the welcome mat.

"I have to ride in a lot of rodeos the next couple of months," Drew explained.

"Can I come to your rodeo?"

Unable to watch her son's hopeful expression crumble, Hallie turned her back on the pair and unlocked the apartment door.

"Not this time, buddy. The rodeos are a long way from Bastrop."

"But I wanna go! I can go, can't I, Mom?" Nick's lip wobbled and Hallie recognized a temper tantrum building.

"You can't miss school." She glanced at Drew, the urge to flee glimmering in his eyes.

Nick threw himself at Drew. "I'm going with my dad." His skinny arms stuck like flypaper to his father's leg.

"I'll stop by again real soon," Drew said.

Drew had better keep his word, or she'd be left with the nasty job of making excuses for him, to spare Nick further hurt.

"No, I wanna go with you!"

"I'm sorry, pal, you can't. Now, be good for your mom."

Hallie pried Nick's arms from Drew's leg and pulled him into the apartment. "That's enough, Nick. Go get ready for bed. I'll be right in."

Nick glared at Drew, then mumbled, "I hate you," before stomping off.

Hallie opened her mouth to reprimand her son, but Drew touched her arm. "Leave him be." Drew shoved a hand through his hair. "I won't let Nick down." His eyes strayed to her mouth and her pulse jumped.

No matter that they shared a son, Drew was the kind of man she didn't want to be involved with, and the fact that he stirred her blood with just a look worried Hallie.

Before she did something she'd regret—like allow him to kiss her—she whispered, "Don't."

"Don't what?"

"Don't look like you want to kiss me," she whispered.

"Why?"

"Because."

"You'll have to come up with a better reason than *because*." His big callused hand cupped her jaw. Then his mouth crushed hers, trapping the air in her lungs. A hint of aftershave clung to his skin, and she nuzzled her nose against his cheek, greedily inhaling his scent. Her body had not forgotten this cowboy or his touch.

Hallie squirmed out of his embrace. "I can't do this again."

"What we shared five years ago is far from over." With one last smoldering look, Drew walked off.

The camper hadn't even left the parking lot and already Hallie's heart ached.

Chapter Six

"Is Dad ever gonna come see me again?" Nick whined.

Hallie stared at her son's solemn face, silently cursing. Drew had kept in touch with Nick by phone, but her son needed more than calls. He needed the reassurance of his father's physical presence. Three weeks, which felt like six months to a four-year-old, had passed since Drew had taken them to eat at Buck's Pizza.

Even though Drew called by seven each evening, Hallie did her best to ignore the clock. Often she ended up pacing the kitchen floor waiting for the phone to ring. Her mother had done the same thing when Hallie's father had been on the road. When the phone hadn't rung, her mother would begin drinking—straight through the night. The next morning Hallie would find her passed out on the couch, hugging the phone to her chest.

Hallie looked forward to Drew's calls if only to reassure herself that he hadn't been injured—Nick would be devastated if Drew got hurt. The shivers that raced down her spine when Drew whispered *darlin'* in her ear meant nothing. She appreciated that he asked about her day and if she or Nick needed anything, but she always answered *no*. She refused to rely on Drew and prayed each evening for the strength and courage to follow through on that pledge.

A crack of thunder rumbled over the apartment complex, and she jumped inside her skin. Parts of Texas, Arkansas and Oklahoma were under flood warnings as a chain of early October storms hammered the states. Hallie glanced at the calendar on the fridge. She'd written down Drew's rodeo schedule because Nick asked her a hundred times a day where his father was. Tomorrow, Drew was riding in Harrison, Arkansas.

"Now what time is it?" Nick sat at the kitchen table drawing pictures.

"Eight-thirty."

"I don't wanna go to bed until Dad calls." He stuck out his lower lip.

After Drew had bullied his way into their lives, Hallie anticipated the three of them would have to make minor adjustments. What had caught her off-guard was Nick's argumentative behavior and uncooperative attitude. She believed Nick's stubbornness was his way of expressing his fear that Drew would change his mind about being his father. Hallie sympathized with her son's anxiety but at the same time resented that he was preoccupied with Drew. She prayed if she bided her time things would return to the way they'd been. Nick would eventually learn that having a rodeo cowboy for a dad wasn't all it was cracked up to be.

"Did you tell Dad not to call?" Nick asked.

Hallie took a deep breath and blamed Nick's hurtful question on the fact that he was overtired. "Of course I didn't." Hallie would be a liar if she didn't admit that she constantly worried how Drew's presence in their lives would impact her relationship with Nick. Jealousy once again made her feel small and vindictive, but it angered her that Drew did nothing but call and her son believed he walked on water. "Let's clean up."

"I don't wanna go to bed." Nick shoved the plastic bin of crayons across the table. The box teetered on the edge, then crashed to the floor. His eyes welled with tears.

"Oh, sweetie." Hallie crouched in front of his chair and pulled him close for a hug.

"Dad forgot me, didn't he?"

Hallie remembered the nights she'd gone to bed feeling unwanted, overlooked and just plain forgotten by her father. She nuzzled Nick's head. "A missed phone call doesn't mean your dad isn't thinking about you."

At moments like this Hallie regretted her decision not to fight Drew when he'd insisted on being involved in Nick's life. Guilt pricked her conscience at the uncharitable thought. Who was she to criticize—until a short while ago she'd never given Drew a choice whether or not to be Nick's father. She had to accept her fair share of the blame for the situation the three of them were stuck in.

"You have me. I'll always be here for you." She hugged Nick. "I'll help you pick up the crayons."

Right then the doorbell rang.

"Dad!" Nick raced from the kitchen.

Hallie rushed after him. "Let me check to see who it is before you open the door." She squinted into the peephole and Drew's blue eyes stared at her.

Nick tugged her shirt. "Who is it?"

"Your dad." Ignoring her clamoring heart, she opened the door.

Drew stood on the welcome mat, weary and soaked to the bone, water dripping off his cowboy hat. Dark smudges beneath his eyes and a five o'clock shadow accentuated his haggard face.

She motioned him inside, then closed the door against the wind and rain.

"Hi, buddy." Drew's mouth curved at the corners, chasing the shadows from his tired eyes.

Nick stared solemnly at Drew. When he remained silent, Drew glanced at Hallie. "What's going on?"

"Nick's been wondering why you haven't stopped by to visit him until now." She wouldn't do Drew any favors if she pretended all was well on the home front. Granted, Drew was new to fatherhood, but he'd better catch on quick if he intended for him and Nick to have a lasting, meaningful relationship.

"I thought you forgot me." Nick edged closer to Hallie and she placed her arm around his shoulders.

"Forgot you? No way." Drew held out a soggy shoe box. "I brought you a present."

"What is it?" Nick knelt on the floor and opened the box. "Cowboy boots!"

The blood rushed from Hallie's face. Since the day her son had discovered his father was a cowboy, Nick had begged and pleaded for a pair of boots—just like his dad's. Feeling threatened by Nick's infatuation with Drew, she'd come up with several reasons why her son didn't need new boots.

Drew chuckled. "Try them on, pardner."

Nick shoved his bare feet into the boots. Grinning

from ear-to-ear he stomped around the room. "Look, Mom. I'm a real cowboy."

Jealous that all it took was a gift from his father and Nick forgot about being upset with Drew, Hallie whispered, "You could have called to tell us you were coming into town tonight." Hadn't he realized she and Nick would worry and wonder when the phone didn't ring?

"I'd planned to be here earlier, but I blew a tire."

"You shouldn't have driven in this weather. There are all kinds of storm warnings posted across the area."

"Can Dad and me watch a movie, Mom?"

"Aren't you competing in Arkansas tomorrow?" Hallie asked.

"My ride isn't until late in the afternoon."

Tomorrow was Saturday. She didn't have to work and Nick could sleep in. "Sure. A movie's okay." Hallie extended the invitation for Nick's sake. *Yeah, right.*

"Mind if I take a quick shower and put my clothes into the dryer?" Drew asked.

"Clean towels are beneath the sink." She pointed to the bathroom down the hallway.

Ten minutes later, Drew entered the kitchen, a pink towel knotted at his waist. She stared at the wall of tanned muscle, cursing the tingle that spread through her stomach. "I'll take those." She snatched the bundle of wet clothes from his arms. "There's a blanket on the couch if you get cold." She tried—really, she did. But her eyes had a will of their own and traveled over his chest, noting the thin line of hair that began at his belly button and disappeared beneath the edge of the towel. Undeterred, she ogled his hairy calves and big bare feet.

He was more…more…everything than she remembered in her dreams.

"Hallie…"

Her gaze collided with Drew's. There was no denying the sizzle that sparked between them. Before she caved in and told him he could spend the night in her bed, she left the room and went to toss his clothes into the washing machine.

HALLIE HAD MADE HERSELF scarce while the guys watched the movie. After doing Drew's laundry, she'd sat on her bed and perused RN magazines. Several minutes passed without hearing any noise from the living room, so she decided to check on Nick and Drew.

The sight of them together tied her heart in knots. No mistaking they were father and son. They shared the same dark, silky hair and square jaws. She slid the remote from Drew's hand, switched the channel to the news, lowered the volume on the TV, then curled up in the chair and studied the sleeping pair.

The bruising and swelling in Drew's left hand had healed. He never complained about his ribs, and Hallie wondered if the injury he'd suffered in August continued to bother him. Drew was past his prime—by rodeo standards. Past the time when his body bounced back easily from injury. He should retire from the sport, yet he never talked about the future. Never mentioned his plans after the finals in December.

"What are you thinking about?"

Startled, Hallie caught Drew watching her. "Wondering if I should wake you," she lied.

"What time is it?" His breath ruffled the hair on the top of Nick's head.

"Almost ten-thirty."

Holding the edges of the towel together, Drew sat up.

"Your clothes are on the counter in the bathroom," she said.

He rubbed a hand down his weary face.

"Did you like the movie?" She pointed to the DVD case on the table.

"I don't remember much. Nick talked my ear off until he fell asleep in the middle of a sentence."

"He missed you." The words darn near choked her.

Drew's face softened as he tucked the blanket around Nick. "I'd better hit the road."

Heavy rain continued to fall outside. "You shouldn't drive in this—"

"I've got a lot of blacktop to cover before tomorrow."

The man was on a suicide mission. Harrison, Arkansas, was ten and a half hours from Bastrop. "You're too tired to drive this late at night."

He flashed a patronizing grin. "I've been driving through the night for years. A few coffee stops along the way and I'll be fine." He headed to the bathroom. "Thanks for doing my laundry." She followed him down the hallway, stopping outside the door.

She forced her eyes to focus on his face—not an easy task with a wall of sexy muscle inches from her nose. "The next time you buy Nick a gift I'd appreciate you asking me first."

He frowned. "I need your permission to buy my son a present?"

"I had good reason not to allow Nick to wear cowboy boots."

Drew closed the distance between them. "Your good reason has *me* written all over it."

"That's not what I—"

"You don't want Nick having anything to do with rodeo or cowboys because I'm a cowboy."

"It's nothing personal."

"Well, it *feels* pretty damn personal." He thumped his fist against his chest. "I don't know why you ran from me five years ago and I haven't any idea what that night in my camper was all about for you." He narrowed his eyes. "I sure as hell don't understand what I did to make you hide my son from me all these years."

Hallie steeled herself against the memories triggered by Drew's words.

He lowered his voice to a rough whisper. "I remember the lost look on your face in the bar. I didn't know what was wrong, but I knew that before the night was through I wanted to erase the sadness from your eyes."

All these years Hallie had convinced herself that her encounter with Drew had been nothing more than a young woman seeking solace after the death of a loved one. But as she stared into Drew's eyes, she acknowledged she'd sought more than comfort from Drew that night.

"Admit it," he said. "What happened between us was special. I felt it. You felt it."

"Okay, it was more than sex." She owed him that—at the very least.

"Then why didn't you tell me you were pregnant?"

She didn't know where to begin.

"I can't make things right until I know what I did wrong."

How like a stubborn cowboy to believe sheer determination and physical strength could fix any problem. "My father was a bull rider."

Drew's eyes widened.

"Rodeo destroyed my family."

"How?"

"My father was always off rodeoing and I saw him only a few times through the years." She sighed. "My mother drank and struggled with bouts of depression. One day I came home from school and found her dead on the couch. She'd taken prescription painkillers and washed them down with a bottle of vodka."

Drew winced. "What happened next?"

"It took months for social services to locate my father. When they did, he said he didn't want a kid tagging along with him from rodeo to rodeo." The cold look in her father's eyes would haunt Hallie's memory forever. "The judge determined I was better off in foster care than being left unsupervised among a bunch of rough-'n'-tumble cowboys.

"In the end everything worked out for the best. My foster mother was the most generous, kind woman I've ever known. She loved me as if she'd given birth to me herself." And when Hallie struggled with her college studies, Margaret O'Fallen had been her biggest cheerleader and refused to allow Hallie to quit school.

Drew tipped her chin and she cringed at the pity in his eyes. "I'm sorry, Hallie. Sorry that you had such a difficult childhood."

She didn't want Drew's sympathy. "I never saw my father again after that day in court. My case worker informed me that he'd died from injuries sustained in a rodeo the year I turned twelve."

"I'm not like your father. I won't run out on Nick."

The words sounded convincing, but it was too early in the game to know for sure that when the going got tough, Drew wouldn't pack his bags and leave for good. Even if he kept his word, there was no way Hallie could protect Nick from the possibility that like her father, Drew might die from doing what he loved best—rodeo. Either way Nick came out the loser.

"Give me a chance to prove myself. That's all I'm asking." Drew stepped back and shut the bathroom door in Hallie's face. A few minutes later he entered the living room. An awkward silence ensued.

"I better go." Drew paused with his hand on the doorknob. "Everything's going to be okay, Hallie."

His words did nothing to calm the queasiness in her stomach.

"Tell Nick I'll call tomorrow after my ride."

"Sure."

The door opened, then shut with a quiet click.

Hallie went to the window overlooking the parking lot and watched Drew's camper drive off into the night. Nothing had changed—Drew was back to chasing rodeos and she was left to deal with Nick's seesawing emotions.

"Hello?"

Hallie's breathless voice drifted through the connection and Drew clutched his cell phone tighter. "It's me."

"Drew? Where are you?"

"Truck stop off the interstate. I'm headed to—"

"Seguin."

He chuckled. "I forgot you wrote down my schedule." Whenever Drew wasn't thinking about rodeo or his next ride, his mind drifted to Hallie and Nick and he imagined where they were and what they were doing at that particular moment in time. The exercise made him feel less alone. "What are you and Nick up to?"

"We just got home from the grocery store. He's tugging on my shirt, so I'd better hand over the phone."

"Hi, Dad!"

His son's shout threatened to deafen Drew. He switched the phone to his other ear. "How are you, buddy?"

"Okay. Are you coming to visit?"

"Not for a while. I'm heading in the opposite direction of Bastrop."

The other end of the connection went silent and guilt slammed into Drew. Hoping to take his son's mind off not visiting, he asked, "How are things at Red Robin?" He'd made the mistake of calling Nick's preschool a day care and Nick had informed him that day cares were for babies. From then on, Drew made a point of using the school's proper name.

"Oh, yeah! I forgot. You gotta come to my play," Nick said.

"What play?"

"I'm gonna be a pumpkin. Mom's sewing my costume and I get to chase after a ghost in the haunted forest."

"Sounds exciting. When's the play?"

"Mom! When's my play?" A few seconds later Nick said, "Friday."

"This coming Friday?"

"This Friday, Mom?"

Hallie shouted, "October seventeenth" from somewhere in the apartment. Drew had already paid his entry fee to ride at the Austin County Fair and Rodeo in Bellville that weekend—an hour and a half from Bastrop. But Drew wouldn't find out when his ride was scheduled until the day of the competition. He couldn't afford to scratch a ride—not this late in the season. He was barely hanging on to fourteenth place in the standings.

"Did you hear, Dad?"

"Yeah, I heard, buddy."

"And there's gonna be cookies and stuff after."

"Sounds like fun."

"Are you gonna come? Please, Dad!"

Feeling hemmed in, Drew said, "I don't know, Nick."

"But Jason thinks I'm making you up."

"He does, huh?"

"Jason says you're not a real cowboy."

A fuzzy feeling warmed Drew's chest. At least his son was impressed with what he did for a living—unlike Hallie. "Let me talk to your mom."

"Hey." Hallie's voice filled his ear.

"This is the first I've heard about a Halloween play."

"Really? I thought I'd mentioned it the last time we spoke."

"No, you didn't." Drew had a hunch she'd neglected

to tell him because she didn't believe he'd make time in his busy schedule for Nick.

Her soft sigh passed through the connection. "I didn't mention the play, because I'd hoped Nick would forget about asking you to come."

Hurt—the deep, bone-aching kind—jarred Drew. "Nick wants me to come."

"We can't count on you to be there with your crazy schedule, can we?"

Drew rubbed his brow and silently cursed Hallie's dead father. He wasn't like her old man. He was better. More committed to Nick than Hallie's father had been to her. What did he have to do to make her believe in him?

Feeling defensive he said, "Maybe I could have changed my schedule if I'd known about the play before now."

"*Maybes* don't work. *Maybe* is as good as *yes* to a four-year-old. Nick would be crushed if you didn't show up. I won't let you hurt him."

Jeez, she knew just what nerve to touch. He'd make the damned play, by God, even if it killed him. "What time do I need to be at the school?"

"Three-thirty."

"Where's this Red Robin located?"

"Five blocks south of the apartment on Hilltop."

Should be easy to find. Nick had explained that the school had a giant red robin painted on the outside of the white brick building.

"He said some kid at school is teasing him."

"Nick's been telling everyone that his father is a

cowboy. Since the kids have never seen you they assume you're Nick's pretend father."

The pressure was building. "Gotta go. I'm running late."

He hesitated before disconnecting the call and was glad when Hallie whispered, "Be careful."

The tension drained from his body. A few kind words from her and he forgot what he'd been all fired up about. "I will."

Come hell or high water, Drew would make the play on Friday. He'd prove to Hallie that he was the kind of man both a child and a woman could count on.

Chapter Seven

"Is he here yet?"

Trying not to allow her agitation to show, Hallie kissed Nick's cheek. "Your costume is crooked." She righted the pumpkin and straightened the green stem behind Nick's neck.

Hallie noticed the teacher corralling the kids in the corner of the room. Several mothers scurried about moving scenery, and reminding the children of their lines.

Ten minutes to curtain call, and Drew was nowhere in sight. He should have phoned her that he wasn't coming, so she could have prepared Nick. "Your dad's probably stuck in traffic."

Nick's shoulders slumped. Her little pumpkin boy looked downright pathetic. Heart aching, she hugged him—that he didn't resist confirmed how upset he was.

Darn Drew for disappointing Nick. "I'll take lots of pictures, so you can show your dad. And Aunt Sharon's here to watch you."

"That's right, Nick. I wouldn't miss your play for anything." Sharon tickled his leg. "I must say, you look dashing in orange tights." Her impersonation of Dracula's voice coaxed a smile out of Nick.

A second later his smile flipped upside down. "I wanted my friends to see Dad."

Careful not to smear the black dots decorating his cheeks, Hallie cupped his face. "I'm sure he has a good reason for missing the play."

"For his sake I hope he does, too," Sharon mumbled beneath her breath.

Hallie kissed Nick's forehead. "Good luck, honey." As soon as he joined his classmates, she motioned to the row of chairs in front. "Let's sit close to the stage."

After picking their seats, Hallie glanced at the classroom door several times, hoping to spot Drew.

"Maybe he really does have a good excuse for not being here," Sharon said.

What if Sharon was right? What if Drew had been hurt during the rodeo, or had gotten into a car accident on the way to Bastrop? Hallie quickly pushed those dark thoughts from her mind. "He let Nick down and I let Nick down because I trusted Drew to be here."

Sharon patted Hallie's hand. "Forget about Drew and enjoy the play."

Hallie was grateful for Sharon's support. "I will." She refused to allow Drew's thoughtlessness to ruin the day. Later, she'd make the infuriating cowboy pay big-time.

The play began and Nick shuffled onto the stage, displaying little enthusiasm for his part. Then he glanced toward the back of the room and suddenly his frown transformed into a smile that rivaled the sun. "Dad!" He waved frantically. "Here I am, Dad!"

Hallie shifted in her seat and spotted Drew hovering in the doorway, hat in hand, covered in dust. His face reddened with embarrassment as heads turned in his direction. He smiled good-naturedly, lifting his Stetson in greeting. The audience chuckled.

Like always, Drew squeaked past another test... barely. Relieved he had shown up, Hallie relaxed and enjoyed the performance. Nick chased a ghost across the stage, then a witch and a goblin joined in the fun as did the rest of the characters.

After a few seconds, the kids stood in their assigned spots and trick-or-treaters walked through the haunted forest. Each time a trick-or-treater asked, "Where are we?" Nick exclaimed, "You're in the haunted forest," then he grinned at Drew.

Not his mother.

Sharon elbowed Hallie in the side. "Smile. You look mad."

When the play ended, Hallie's cheeks hurt from grinning. She and Sharon joined the milling parents by the stage and waited for Nick. "Honey, I'm so proud—"

As if they were invisible, Nick flew past, dodging bodies. "I knew you'd come! I knew you'd come!"

Swallowing the ache building in her throat, Hallie ignored the stares of several mothers and willed the tears away that blurred her vision. It wasn't fair that she got shoved aside when Drew showed up.

"He didn't disappoint Nick." Sharon flashed a sympathetic smile. "That's the important thing, right?"

"Right." No damage had been done. This time. *But what about next time? Or the time after that?* She and

Sharon cut through the crowd and joined Nick and Drew at the back of the classroom.

"You did great, buddy. That's some costume." Drew tugged Nick's pumpkin stem.

Hallie sucked in a quiet breath when she got her first close look at Drew's face. Lines of fatigue stood out in stark contrast to the dark circles beneath his eyes.

"Hallie," he said.

She didn't trust herself not to pick a fight, so she responded in kind. "Drew."

"Hello, Sharon."

"Drew," Sharon said.

Talk about awkward.

"I'm gonna get Dad some cookies." Nick dashed off to join the other children filling their plates with Halloween goodies.

"I'm hungry for cookies, too." Sharon excused herself, leaving Hallie alone with Drew.

"Nick was really upset when he thought you were going to miss the play." The barb slipped out before Hallie could stop it.

"I would have been here sooner but the camper broke down."

Drew must have put over a hundred thousand miles on the vehicle. Did he expect it to run forever? He might have a legitimate excuse for being late, but that didn't get him off the hook with Hallie. "How did you get here?"

"Brody gave me a lift."

What if Brody hadn't been there? In Hallie's mind, Drew's tardiness proved that he refused to make his son a priority in his life, which would eventually lead to bigger problems as Nick grew older. "Where's the camper now?"

"Repair shop in Bellville. Brody'll take me back there after I visit with Nick."

A single mother of one of Nick's classmates batted her eyelashes at Drew, and Hallie stepped sideways, blocking the woman's view. "How long before Brody picks you up?"

"I've got time to take you and Nick out for a bite to eat." He nodded toward the crowd around the food. "Unless you and Nick already have plans with Sharon."

"No. Sharon has to get back to the hospital." Her eyes roamed over him and despite his obvious exhaustion her heart raced. "You're not dressed for a restaurant."

"I didn't have time to shower and change after my ride." He rubbed a hand over his shirt and dust particles floated in the air.

"You might as well come back to the apartment. While you clean up, I'll wash your clothes." Hallie's home was becoming Drew's personal diner and Laundromat.

"Sounds good, thanks."

"Here, Dad." Nick shoved a paper plate filled with frosted pumpkin cookies and cellophane-wrapped chocolate ghosts at his father. "I told my teacher—Ms. Brewer—you'd be real hungry after bustin' broncs."

Drew chuckled. "What did Ms. Brewer say about that?"

"She said she likes cowboys."

Ms. Brewer was single.

"Why don't you show your dad the Halloween picture you painted in art class?" Hallie followed father and son at a distance as the pair admired the artwork displayed on the room walls. After a couple of minutes, Nick introduced the other boys and their fathers to Drew.

Feeling left out, Hallie stood to the side, resenting Drew's presence.

He'd made Nick's day.

But he'd ruined hers.

WRAPPING A TOWEL around his waist, Drew stepped from the shower. The hot water had worked out the kinks from his tired muscles, but his ribs ached. He'd been thrown into the rails today and already his side was turning black and blue. Brody had offered to take him to the hospital for an X-ray, but there had been no time—not if he'd wanted to make it to Nick's school for the opening of the play.

A knock sounded at the door. "Who is it?"

"Mom says you need this," Nick answered in a muffled tone.

Drew tightened the towel around his waist, then opened the door. Slicker than a greased pig, his son slipped past him.

"Here." Nick held up a disposable razor and a can of women's shaving cream. "Mom says you can use her stuff." Nick climbed onto the counter. "What happened?" He pointed to the bruising along Drew's rib cage.

"I bumped into a post."

"Does it hurt?"

"Nah. It'll be fine in a day or two."

Nick averted his face. Where had the happy-go-lucky pumpkin gone? "What's wrong?" Drew asked.

Nick shrugged.

The kid hadn't stopped chatting the whole way home after the play. What had caused the change in his demeanor? Maybe Drew wasn't cut out for fatherhood. He had no experience handling these awkward moments. "If everything's okay, then why the long face?"

"I thought you were gonna miss my play."

"I promised I'd be there, didn't I?"

Nick nodded.

"What else is on your mind?"

"Mom said we're going to the zoo with Dr. Feller but I wanna go to the zoo with you."

Damn. He couldn't catch a break. Nick expected to be a priority in his father's life—and he should be—but until the finals were over in December, Drew couldn't be there for his son. Still, Drew needed to find a way to spend more time with Nick. He couldn't stand the thought of Hallie's *friend* Dr. Feller taking over the role of father in Nick's life.

"I wish we could go to the zoo together, buddy, but I've got to get the camper fixed before my next rodeo."

"Are you gonna bust broncs forever?"

The forlorn note in Nick's voice stabbed Drew in the heart. "Nope. After I win in December, I'm hanging up my spurs for good. Then you and I will spend a lot more time together." He didn't want to consider what would happen if he didn't win the title in Vegas.

"Can I have some?" Nick pointed to the can of shaving cream.

Drew squirted a dollop of foam in the center of the

boy's small palm. Nick sniffed the glob. "Smells like flowers."

"Maybe we should stick you in a vase." Drew flicked a dab of shaving cream at Nick.

"Dad!" Nick giggled. "How come you put this stuff on your face?"

Relieved his son's gloom-and-doom expression had lightened, Drew said, "It softens my whiskers."

"Let me feel." Nick rubbed Drew's cheek. "You're prickly."

"Not for long." Drew lathered his cheeks and neck, then began shaving.

"I wanna be just like you when I grow up," Nick said.

Drew remembered the times his old man had said Drew would never amount to anything. But Nick's words made him feel like he finally was something special. His heart swelled.

"Dad."

"What?"

"I did something bad."

Drew raised an eyebrow. "How bad?" He rinsed the razor and patted his face dry with a towel.

"I snuck out of my room and…"

"And?"

"Mom told Aunt Sharon…"

Drew didn't want to know what his son overheard. "Go on, I'm listening."

"Mom said you're gonna break your promises to me." Nick's eyes welled with tears. "Are you?"

That Hallie doubted his ability to be a steady influence in their son's life didn't surprise Drew, but shoot,

Nick didn't need to know his mother felt that way. Drew felt the pressure building again. One screwup and Hallie would ban him from Nick's life. Drew had shown up for the play today, but because he'd been a few minutes late, he'd earned a black mark in Hallie's book.

"I'm trying real hard to keep my promises, buddy." He ruffled Nick's hair. How the heck did he tell his son he wouldn't let him down, when he didn't know if he would or not? Drew had believed he was doing the right thing by phoning Nick every night. But a call hundreds of miles away wasn't the same as being there. His son needed the reassurance of his father's physical presence—the one thing Drew couldn't give him right now.

"Mom, when's Dad gonna wake up?" Nick asked when he entered the kitchen.

An hour and a half ago, Drew had sat in the chair to watch TV with Nick and then had fallen asleep. Hallie hadn't had the heart to wake him. Instead of eating out, she'd decided to cook a meal at home and allow Drew to rest before Brody picked him up.

A shower and a shave had improved Drew's appearance, but the careful way he moved around the apartment convinced her that he'd reinjured his ribs. She wanted to urge him to see a doctor but knew he'd refuse. If Drew kept pushing himself he'd risk serious injury. "Why don't you play in your room until dinner's ready, then you can wake your dad."

Nick obeyed, mumbling beneath his breath as he left the kitchen.

Roast chicken warmed in the oven and gravy bubbled

on the stove. Hallie strained the potatoes and retrieved the mixer. After adding a stick of butter and milk to the pot, she flipped the mixer on high and whipped the potatoes.

"Mmm...smells good."

Drew's sleep-slurred voice startled Hallie, and she lifted the beaters, splattering bits of potato against the wall.

"Sorry." Drew stepped back, allowing her to draw in a much-needed breath. "I thought I was taking everyone out to eat."

She finished mashing the potatoes—not an easy task when Drew's stare burned the back of her neck. "I already had supper planned in case..."

"You don't have much faith in me." Hurt shadowed his eyes.

Hallie refused to respond for fear she'd reveal her conflicting emotions. She'd wanted Drew to make Nick's play because she loved her son and hated to see him disappointed. Yet, she'd also secretly hoped Drew wouldn't show because she wanted to be the hero today. The one who was there for Nick. The one he could count on. Just the thought made her ashamed.

"Nick thinks you're some kind of god." She carried the potatoes to the table. "He's so little. So vulnerable." She jutted her chin. "I'm his mother. I have to protect him the best I know how."

"And what about you?" Drew blocked her path to the stove. "Who's going to protect you—" he skimmed his knuckles across her cheek and she shivered "—from me?"

The urge to allow herself to care about Drew tugged

at her heart. But long ago she vowed to find a man who'd put her and Nick first in his life. Drew wasn't that man. "Would you tell Nick to wash up?"

The heat in Drew's eyes banked, and he left the room. Hallie hated that she'd hurt his feelings, especially when deep down she yearned for a dark room and few hours in his arms. In the long run, they were both better off resisting their attraction to one another.

A half hour later Hallie sat at the kitchen table, awed by the amount of food Drew had consumed. He'd complimented her cooking throughout the meal while devouring three helpings of everything.

"Hey, Dad?"

"What?"

"Do I have a grandma and a grandpa?"

The fork slipped from Hallie's fingers, banging against the plate. Their relationship was tangled and complicated enough without adding more people to the mix.

"You have a grandmother," Drew said. "Your grandfather died a long time ago."

Nick's eyes lit with curiosity. "When can I see my grandma?"

"That's up to your mom."

Great. Now she'd be the bad guy again if she didn't allow Nick to meet Drew's mother.

"Where does my grandma live?"

"In a small town north of San Antonio."

"Do I got lots of cousins? My friend Jimmy gots a million cousins."

Drew grinned. "Sorry, buddy. No cousins."

Did that mean Drew was an only child? Suddenly Hallie was reminded of how little she knew about him.

"When can we see my grandma?" Nick asked Hallie.

"I don't know, honey. Right now, I need you to pick up the toys in your room while I clean up the kitchen."

"But Dad's gonna throw the football with me. Right, Dad?" Nick's anxious expression looked suspicious.

This was the first Hallie had heard of any football game. "It's too dark outside to throw the ball."

Drew clasped Nick's shoulder. "You should have asked me earlier. We could have gone outside then."

"You were sleeping and Mom said I had to leave you alone."

"We'll toss the ball around the next time I visit."

Head hanging, Nick shuffled from the kitchen.

"Thank you," Hallie said.

"For what?"

"For backing me up." She gathered the dirty plates.

Drew helped clear the table. "No big deal."

"Actually, your support is a big deal. Nick's testing us. Trying to figure out who has more authority and which parent is easier to manipulate."

"Does he give you a hard time when I'm on the road?"

Admitting she had trouble with their son wasn't easy. "Nick's been difficult to handle," she said. "The telephone calls help."

"How so?"

Hallie struggled to collect her thoughts. Each time Drew passed her on the way to the sink, she caught a whiff of his clean scent and the smell played havoc with her concentration. "The evenings you're late phoning, Nick blames me. He accuses me of not wanting you to call or of me telling you not to contact him."

"That's ridiculous. You have no control over—"

She held up a hand. "When you're not here, Nick has to have a reason."

"You don't defend yourself?"

His incredulous tone irked her. "I don't say a word either way."

"Why?"

"I know from experience that it's better if Nick believes I told you to stay away than for him to assume you don't want to be with him."

Drew's eyes darkened. "That's not fair to you."

What choice did Hallie have? She'd spent her childhood believing *she* had been the reason her father seldom came home. Then when he'd handed her over to the state after her mother had died, Hallie had believed there was something wrong with her and that's why her father had given her up so easily.

"Tell me how to help," Drew said.

"There's no easy fix, unless you plan to retire from rodeo. Today."

Drew shoved his hands into the front pockets of his jeans and leaned against the refrigerator. "That's out of the question."

"I try to envision you and Nick together ten years from now." Her attempt at a smile fell short. "But my mind is blank."

"I'm sorry this has been hard on you."

She believed him—simply because he'd said so.

How could she protect her heart from the man when everything in her screamed to allow him closer?

"I'll visit more often," he said.

"Nick would appreciate that." Tears sprang to her eyes and she silently cursed. Embarrassed by the frailty of her emotions, she turned away and began loading the dishwasher.

A moment later, Drew's hands rested on her hips. She froze as his arms moved around her, his fingers splaying across her stomach. With the slightest pressure, he turned her toward him. Her nose bumped his chest. The scent of laundry detergent surrounded her.

"I need to check my schedule, but maybe I can squeeze in an extra visit between rodeos in November."

"That would be nice." The more she saw of Drew, the more she wanted to be with him.

His bold stare moved to her breasts and Hallie closed her eyes, envisioning his hands on her body... his mouth on hers. If she concentrated hard enough she could almost hear his tender words whispering in her ear. When she opened her eyes, Drew was watching her. The faint rumble in his throat sent sweet shivers racing down her spine. His lips crushed hers and she moaned in pleasure, the sound growing louder when he caressed her breast. Could he feel the pounding of her heart beneath his hand?

"Yuck!"

Their eyes opened and for an eternal second Drew and Hallie stared at each other in shock. Then Drew stepped back and faced Nick. "Hey, sport."

"Kissing's gross."

"Your dad was just saying goodbye," Hallie said.

Get 2 Books FREE!

Harlequin® Books,
publisher of women's fiction,
presents

GET 2 BOOKS

We'd like to send you two *Harlequin American Romance*® novels absolutely free! Accepting them puts you under no obligation to purchase any more books.

HOW TO GET YOUR
2 FREE BOOKS AND 2 FREE GIFTS

1. Return the reply card today, and we'll send you two *Harlequin American Romance* novels, absolutely free! We'll even pay the postage!

2. Accepting free books places you under no obligation to buy anything, ever. Whatever you decide, the free books and gifts are yours to keep, free!

3. We hope that after receiving your free books you'll want to remain a subscriber, but the choice is yours—to continue or cancel, any time at all!

EXTRA BONUS

You'll also get two free mystery gifts! (worth about $10)

FREE!

If offer card is missing, write to: The Reader Service, P.O. Box 1867, Buffalo, NY 14240-1867 or visit www.ReaderService.com

BUSINESS REPLY MAIL

FIRST-CLASS MAIL   PERMIT NO. 717   BUFFALO, NY

POSTAGE WILL BE PAID BY ADDRESSEE

THE READER SERVICE
PO BOX 1867
BUFFALO NY 14240-9952

NO POSTAGE
NECESSARY
IF MAILED
IN THE
UNITED STATES

Drew checked his watch. "Brody's probably waiting outside."

"Am I gonna get to see my grandma?"

Hallie stiffened at the question. She waited for Drew to make eye contact with her but he focused on Nick and said, "I'm riding in Helotes next weekend. You want to come watch?"

"Yeah!"

Hallie balled her hands into fists.

"I'll take you behind the chutes and introduce you to all the cowboys, and you can see the horses up close."

"Say good night to your father, Nick." Hallie wanted to smack the grin off Drew's face.

Nick crossed the room and lifted his arms. Instead of picking him up, Drew went down on one knee and gave Nick a hug—a telltale sign of injured ribs. "Be good for your mom."

"Okay."

As soon as Nick left the room, Hallie whispered, "Don't ever do that again."

"Do what?"

"Make plans in front of Nick without discussing them with me first."

Drew shoved a hand through his hair, leaving the strands on end. "What's wrong with watching his father compete?"

"Nick and I already had plans that weekend." At Drew's frown she explained. "Mark is taking us to the San Antonio zoo."

"I think Nick would rather go to a rodeo than the zoo."

"That's beside the point."

"The rodeo's close to my mother's house. It would be a good chance for you all to meet."

"You told your mother about Nick?"

He nodded. "She's eager to meet you both."

Not only did Hallie have to watch in fear when Drew competed at the rodeo, but she'd also have to field questions from his mother about why she'd kept Nick a secret all these years.

Yee-ha!

Chapter Eight

Hallie glanced at the piece of paper in her hand—directions to Aimee Rawlins's home in Hollywood Park, nestled in the Hill Country foothills north of San Antonio.

"Are we there yet?" Nick asked.

"Almost." They'd been in the car an hour and fifteen minutes and Hallie swore her son had repeated the question fifty times since they'd left the apartment after breakfast. She eyed the street signs as she drove down the main drag of the quaint town. "Third Street." She flipped on the blinker.

"Is this where my grandma lives?"

"Be on the lookout for your dad's camper." Drew planned to meet Hallie at his mother's before taking them to the rodeo.

"There it is!" Nick's shout startled Hallie, but she managed not to slam on the brakes.

The camper was parked in front of a white single-story ranch house with blue shutters on the windows. A glider sat in the front yard beneath a large oak tree. A fake family of deer rested nearby. Hallie pulled into the drive.

Nick unsnapped his seat belt. "There's Dad." He bolted from the car, cut across the lawn and raced up the porch steps. Drew twirled him in the air, then set him on his feet. A moment later, an older woman stepped out of the home and smiled at Nick.

Drew's mother was short and round—like Mrs. Claus. Gray hair in a bun, she wore a pink blouse with a pair of navy slacks. Whatever Nick said made the woman laugh and she ruffled his hair. Her obvious joy at meeting her grandson added to Hallie's guilty feelings at keeping Nick all to herself.

Taking a deep breath, she left the car, waving a hello as she approached the group.

"Mom, this is Hallie Sutton. Hallie, this is my mother, Aimee Rawlins."

"Nice to meet you, Mrs. Rawlins."

Drew's mother offered a cool smile. "Please call me Aimee." She took Nick by the hand. "C'mon inside. I've got fresh sticky buns hot out of the oven."

Hallie didn't blame Aimee for the tepid reception. Like Drew, maybe with time she'd forgive Hallie for keeping her grandson a secret all these years.

"We've got a couple of hours before we leave for the fairgrounds," Drew said.

"I'm not sure Nick can behave himself that long." *And I'm not up to a two-hour interrogation from your mother.*

Drew grasped her hand and squeezed. "Relax. Mom's thrilled that you and Nick are here."

Nick, of course, but not Hallie. A short while later, after eating their fill of sticky buns, Nick and Drew went outside to toss the football around. Hallie remained in the kitchen with Aimee.

"Nick's a precious boy." Aimee topped off Hallie's coffee cup.

"I don't know what I would do without him."

"Drew tells me your parents are deceased."

Hallie nodded. "No sisters or brothers, either."

"I suffered complications after Drew was born and couldn't have any more children. You can imagine how excited I was to learn I had a grandson." Aimee's stare cut through Hallie.

"You're probably wondering why I never told Drew about Nick."

"I would be lying if I said I wasn't interested in hearing your reasons for keeping my grandson from his family." Hallie opened her mouth, but Aimee held up her hand. "Before you say a word, I want you to know I love my son. He's not without faults, but he didn't deserve what you did to him." Aimee brushed her hands down her apron. "There. I had my say and I won't speak of it again."

If Hallie's throat hadn't swelled shut she would have apologized. Right now it was all she could do to hold back the tears.

"Family is important to me," Aimee said. "Regardless of what happens between you and Drew, I hope you'll allow me to be a part of Nick's life. I'd love to spoil him rotten."

Wiping away a stray tear from her cheek, Hallie whispered, "Of course." Now that she knew where Drew's mother lived, there was no reason she and Nick couldn't drive to Hollywood Park for an occasional visit.

"My sister Helen is taking care of her grandchildren in Dallas while her daughter and son-in-law are in Hawaii. Helen has two granddaughters, Emma and Elizabeth, who are close to Nick in age, and a grandson Kyle, who's twelve. I'd love for all the kids to meet sometime. They'd have fun together." Aimee poured herself a cup of coffee and joined Hallie at the table.

"Nick's excited to see his daddy ride today," Aimee said.

"I know."

"You don't sound very enthused."

"I don't have a high opinion of rodeo." Hallie cleared her throat. "It has nothing to do with Drew."

"Drew said your father was a bull rider."

"Rodeo was more important to my father than his wife or daughter." Hallie winced at the critical note in her voice.

"Sounds like your parents had a stressful relationship."

Maybe a little information about her family would help Aimee understand—not forgive—why Hallie had kept Nick a secret from Drew. "My mother committed suicide when I was seven, because she couldn't accept that my father loved rodeo more than her."

For the first time since Hallie had arrived, Aimee's expression softened. "I'm sorry about your mother."

"My father relinquished custody of me to the state and I never saw him again."

"I met Drew's daddy, J.T., at a rodeo. He was a bare-back rider." Her mouth curved in a soft smile. "J.T. was so handsome and such a braggart. We were both young and foolish. When I turned up pregnant, he was devastated." Aimee's smile faltered. "It was never the same between us after that, but I was lucky compared to your mother. J.T. stuck by my side."

"I realize that keeping Nick a secret from Drew was wrong. But after the way my father treated me and my mother..." Hallie shook her head. "I refused to put my child through that kind of pain."

"My son deserves a chance to prove he's not like your father."

"Trust doesn't come easy for me, but I'm trying."

"That's understandable." Aimee sipped her coffee. "J.T. took the high road and married me—but only after I pressured him. I didn't want to shame my parents. I thought things would get better after Drew was born, but J.T. resented having to give up rodeo for a baby." She sighed. "After a few years I told J.T. to go back to riding broncs, but by then he'd lost his edge. He worked the rest of his years in my father's grocery store and died a bitter man."

"Why did Drew become involved in rodeo?"

Tears welled in Aimee's eyes. "My son is bustin' broncs for all the wrong reasons. He's trying to win J.T.'s approval."

"But his father's..." *Dead.*

"Drew should play an active role in Nick's life. My son needs a reason to quit rodeo."

A tiny part of Hallie's heart—the part that had allowed Drew to sneak past her defenses all those years ago—insisted she and Nick were reason enough for the cowboy to retire his spurs. Maybe it was just as well Drew hadn't figured that out yet, because Hallie didn't have the courage to risk her heart on a rodeo cowboy.

POPCORN.

Hallie expected the pungent smell of sweat, animals and manure to assail her when they entered the arena at the Helotes Festival Association Rodeo early Saturday afternoon. Instead, the scent of buttery popcorn greeted her nose.

After her heart-to-heart chat with Aimee earlier in the day, Hallie believed she and Drew had suffered a similar fate—that of a child yearning for a father's approval but never receiving it. Hallie owed it to herself and Nick to be more understanding of Drew's obsession with rodeo.

Rodeo aside, Hallie acknowledged that Drew was honorable, dedicated and hard-working—a better man by far than her father had been. More importantly, she'd witnessed the way Drew looked at Nick—he loved his son. At those times Hallie felt particularly vulnerable to Drew, fantasizing that if he quit rodeo, the three of them could become a real family.

Bug-eyed and mesmerized by the hustle and bustle of rodeo fans, Nick held tight to Drew's hand. Her son's interest in cowboys worried Hallie. He saw larger-than-life heroes strutting around in big hats, flashing shiny buckles, and wearing fancy boots. He didn't see the heartache, the pain or the injuries that went along with the sport. And Nick didn't notice the toll a grueling rodeo schedule was taking on his father.

That Drew was a favorite among fans didn't escape Hallie's notice. Men stopped to shake his hand. Kids asked for his autograph. Females from ten to fifty smiled and flirted with him, which woke the green-eyed monster inside Hallie. Forcing the jealous feelings aside, she reminded herself that she had no claim on Drew and didn't want one.

"Will you keep an eye on this while I sign in?" Drew set his gear bag on the floor near the restrooms.

"Sure," Hallie said.

Drew glanced at Nick. "Want to tag along?"

"Yeah!"

After Drew and Nick walked off, Hallie eyed the horse in a livestock pen across the way. The gelding was a deep chestnut-brown with bold white markings on his back. She was so enthralled with the animal she didn't notice she had company.

"Ma'am."

Hallie jumped inside her skin and almost landed on her fanny when her foot became tangled in the handles of the gear bag. The cowboy looked familiar. "I'm sorry, have we met before?"

"Brody Murphy. Drew's rodeo buddy."

Ah, the man who reminded her of a Hollywood movie star. "How's the wrist?" She motioned to the bandage wrapped around his hand and forearm.

"Fine." The bull rider rolled his shoulders as if uncomfortable in her presence.

"Drew should be back in a minute," she said.

"I wanted to speak with you, not Drew."

"Oh?" She smiled, but Brody's expression remained sober. "Is something the matter?"

"Ever since Drew found out he had a son, he's lost his edge."

"I don't understand."

Brody paced in front of Hallie, then stopped. "I bet

he didn't tell you he almost got his hand torn off a while back."

Hallie blanched at the memory of Drew sitting at her kitchen table with his bruised and swollen hand packed in ice. Had the incident been more serious than he'd let on?

"He's wearing himself out trying to squeeze in time for the boy between rodeos."

"Drew calls and visits us because he wants to. *Not* because I tell him to." Hallie embraced her anger— better anger than fear.

"If Drew doesn't get his act together he'll end up busting his leg in five places or worse breaking his neck from a bad fall."

The blood drained from her face.

"He's getting up there in age," Brody continued. "This year might be his last chance to win the big one. He really needs your support."

Hallie didn't want to believe she and Nick were a greater danger to Drew than the wild broncs he rode.

"In order to move up in the standings and make it to Vegas in December, Drew's gonna have to ride in a whole lot of rodeos."

Right then Drew and Nick walked around the corner. When Drew casually draped an arm over her shoulder, the bull rider's face turned ruddy.

"Hey, Brody, care to join us for a bite to eat later this afternoon?"

"Thanks, but I've got plans. Good luck today." Brody walked off.

"Wonder what's got him riled up?"

"Maybe he's nervous," Hallie said. If Brody had told

the truth…that trying to rodeo and be a father to Nick was affecting Drew's performance, then Hallie had to be more supportive—for Nick's sake. Her son would never be the same if his father suffered a debilitating injury or worse.

"Let's go see the horses." Drew grabbed the gear bag and led the way to the stock pens. He squatted next to Nick and pointed to a black gelding. "That fella weighs almost two thousand pounds."

Nick stared in awe at the horse.

The animal's muscular haunches and massive girth explained why cowboys waddled around bow-legged.

"Can I pet him?" When Nick reached between the bars of the pen, Drew clamped a hand on his shoulder.

"No, son. He's not all that friendly. He wouldn't be a good bucking horse if he liked people." Drew stood. "Let's find your seats."

The arena stands buzzed with excitement, but the only thing humming inside Hallie was anxiety. Drew pulled them aside near their assigned row. He lifted Nick into his arms. "If I fall off my horse, don't worry. I'll hop right up, okay?"

"Don't get hurt, Dad."

"I won't, buddy." He set Nick down. "Wait for your mom in your seat." Once the clowns distracted Nick, Drew turned to Hallie. "What's wrong? You've been really quiet. Did Brody say something to upset you?"

"No. Just be careful, okay?" She forced a smile.

"How about a good-luck kiss?" Eyes smoldering, he lowered his head. Without conscious thought she met him halfway. The tip of his tongue teased the corner of her mouth, lingering until she opened to him. His kiss was firm, yet gentle. Demanding, yet giving.

I'm scared for you, Drew.

His tongue retreated from her mouth, and he nibbled her lower lip.

I'm proud of you.

He nuzzled her cheek.

Please give up rodeo for Nick.

His lips brushed her forehead.

Win, Drew, win!

His mouth found hers again. She tasted fear—hers or Drew's, she didn't know.

Had Brody been right? Moments from now would Drew think of her and Nick watching in the stands instead of focusing on his ride?

Drew ended the kiss, then walked off, leaving Hallie more uncertain about where Drew fit into her and Nick's future.

HALLIE AND NICK sat five rows up from the arena floor—too close for comfort. Music blared from the sound system as the announcer paid tribute to the flag girls riding into the arena wearing matching red, white and blue sequined costumes.

During the anthem Hallie scanned the cowboy-ready area. She was about to give up hope of finding Drew when she caught a flash of black and red moving among the cowboys. Even though he stood taller than most men he looked small next to the gelding in the chute. As if he felt her stare, he searched the stands. His eyes locked with hers and he tipped his hat before turning away.

The announcer's craggy voice introduced the rodeo

clowns. "Folks, we got us the best of the best in clowns tonight. How about a big welcome for brothers Bobbles and Bibbles from Wichita, Kansas."

Nick watched the clowns goof off for a few moments, then asked, "When's Dad gonna ride?"

Hallie opened the program and scanned the schedule of events. "Saddle-bronc riding is first."

"I know another name for bronc," Nick boasted.

"Really?"

"A mean sumbitch."

"Nick!"

He pointed to the milling cowboys behind the chutes. "That's what they called 'em."

If *sumbitch* was the worst word Nick picked up after a day at the rodeo Hallie would be grateful.

"Ladies and gents, welcome to the twenty-ninth annual Helotes Festival Association Rodeo! We got us a pot of money today big enough to boil a bull in."

The roar of the crowd carried ominous undertones. "The top ride in each category walks away with five thousand dollars."

Five thousand dollars! Hallie presumed the cowboys collected a few hundred bucks for a win.

"First up is rodeo's classic event, the saddle-bronc competition. The cowboy's gotta keep his seat for eight seconds before getting tossed. Watch their legs now. They're gonna try rollin' their spurs along the animal's neck to put a little fire under the hooves!"

Praying Drew's ride would go off without a hitch, Hallie grabbed Nick's hand and squeezed.

"Ouch." Nick yanked his fingers loose from her grip.

"Sorry," she mumbled.

"All eyes on chute number seven. Riley Fitzgerald from Lexington, Kentucky, is comin' out on Sundance."

By the time Hallie located the chute, the horse and cowboy were halfway across the arena. Fitzgerald made the buzzer and the crowd cheered loudly.

"An eighty-one! Not bad for an eight-second workday. For those of you greenhorns out there who ain't never been to a rodeo, the cowboy earns points for his ride and the animal earns points, too. The meaner the bronc the better the score."

The next rider didn't make the buzzer. Hallie winced when he sailed over the horse's head, bouncing twice against the ground before sliding to a stop in the dirt.

"Let's give a howdy-doody welcome to our two pickup men this afternoon. Jerry Weston and Ralph Kroder."

"What's a pickup men?" Nick asked as the cowboys rode around the arena, waving their hats.

"I think they help the cowboy when he falls down," she said.

"Ladies and gentleman! Chute five! Daniel Montgomery, from Houston, is about to tangle with Black Beauty, the newest bucker on the circuit." The horse exploded from the chute with his head swinging and his feet spread wide. Three solid bucks and the cowboy slid to the ground. A collective gasp rippled through the stands when the animal's hooves barely missed the contestant's head. The pickup men crowded the bronc, forcing the animal away from the fallen rider.

Three more cowboys came and went—two earning

scores in the high seventies. The crowd's enthusiasm waned, then Drew's turn arrived.

"This is the ride we've been waitin' for, folks! Drew Rawlins is about to tangle with Windjammer, a veteran bronc that can throw the best of cowboys!"

Shocked by the deafening roar of the crowd, Hallie glanced around in amazement. Until this moment, she'd never given any real thought to how good Drew might be.

Pride swelled inside her and she feared her chest might burst. That she was proud of a man who made a living risking his life didn't make sense. But Drew had fathered her child, and because of that simple fact, he'd already claimed a piece of her heart. Pride waned as she recalled her conversation with Brody and her stomach curled into a tight ball.

"If y'all remember, Rawlins took a nasty horse hoof to the chest at the rodeo over in Bastrop this past August."

A vision of Drew in the E.R. buttoning his shirt with shaking hands flashed before Hallie's eyes.

"But Rawlins says he's good as new and ready to ride!"

Hallie's eyes were glued to Drew as he eased a leg over the back of the bronc. The animal balked and she held her breath.

Nick tugged her shirtsleeve. "I can't see Dad!"

She pointed across the arena where Drew wrapped the rein around his left hand. Head bent, he slid low in the saddle and leaned back. A second later the gate opened and Windjammer burst from the metal prison like a cannonball straight into the air. In a move that defied logic, the front of the horse swung right at the same time the back swung left. Such a violent twist should have snapped the animal's spine.

The ride lasted an eternity, but Drew held on for eight seconds. The buzzer sounded and applause thundered through the stands as Drew struggled to dismount. Horse and rider moved in slow motion before Hallie's eyes as Windjammer continued to buck. It was only a matter of time before Drew ran out of strength to hold on.

The pickup men forced the gelding against the rails, but the bronc broke loose. A second later, Drew freed his hand but Windjammer registered one last protest that sent Drew head first toward the ground.

Hallie's heart stopped beating.

"Daaaaad!" Nick's scream echoed in her ears as she stared in horror.

Drew twisted his hips at the last second—the movement sending his shoulder, instead of his skull, slamming into the dirt.

"He's okay, honey. He's okay." Nick's trembling body frightened Hallie as much as Drew's fall.

The pickup men escorted the gelding out of the arena and Drew slowly got to his feet. He favored his left shoulder as he staggered a few steps, then regained his balance. With a weaving stride he walked over to what was left of his hat and used the toe of his boot to flip it up off the ground. He waved his Stetson and the fans erupted into another frenzied roar.

"There you have it, folks. The ride of the day. How about that cowboy, Drew Rawlins!"

"They like Dad," Nick said.

"They sure do." She tugged Nick's hand. "Let's find

your father." She had to see for herself that Drew was all right. It had been impossible to tell from the stands if he'd dislocated his shoulder.

As they headed for the chutes, the announcer bellowed. "Drew Rawlins scored an eighty-three! Ooowee! That's good enough for first place. If Rawlins keeps riding like this he just might make it to the NFR in Vegas!"

Vegas, my butt. Any more dismounts like today and Drew wouldn't be riding next week, let alone next month.

"Be on the lookout for your father." Drew was nowhere in sight and Hallie's panic increased. Had he been rushed to the first-aid station? A moment later she located Drew in the center of a gathering of cowboys.

Her body trembled with anger and fear. He'd risked his life, and for a few moments she'd known what it would feel like to lose him. Yet there he stood, back-slapping with a bunch of redneck, ill-mannered, tobacco-chewing cowpokes. Drew Rawlins was nothing more than an eight-second heartache.

He glanced up and their eyes met. She'd never seen such exhilaration in his expression. She wished she—and not rodeo—had put that smile on his face.

Chapter Nine

"This year might be his last chance to win the big one. He really needs your support."

Brody's words echoed through Hallie's mind as she stared at the clock. Six fifty-five. Drew had yet to call. Only a week had passed since she and Nick had attended the Helotes rodeo. The seven days had felt like a month.

She poured herself a third cup of coffee. She could blame her accelerated heartbeat on too much caffeine, but the moment she closed her eyes, images of Drew flying off Windjammer and hitting the ground sent her blood pressure skyrocketing. After witnessing the danger Drew put himself in week after week, Hallie worried about the stubborn cowboy twenty-four hours a day.

Each night between supper and Nick's bedtime her anxiety escalated. When the phone didn't ring, she worried. When it did ring, she worried it might be Brody calling with bad news—news she'd have to pass along to her son.

Hallie fretted about the emotional toll Drew's long absences were taking on Nick. He missed his father and asked Drew each time he called, "When you coming home, Dad?" Then after Nick hung up, he'd beg Hallie to take him to Drew's next rodeo. Saying no to her son was doubly difficult when she missed Drew almost as much as Nick.

What surprised her most was that she enjoyed the sense of family she'd felt when they'd attended the Helotes rodeo. For one day they'd behaved as a real family. But the day had ended with everyone going their separate ways, reminding Hallie that she and her son came in a distant second to rodeo.

She yearned to believe she'd overcome her childhood fear of abandonment; her mother, deciding Hallie wasn't enough to live for if she couldn't be with her husband; Hallie's father viewing her as an obstacle in the path of his rodeo career. The fonder Hallie's heart grew of Drew, the greater her insecurities.

The Helotes rodeo had proved a wake-up call for Hallie. Television interviews, fan autographs and the announcer's accolades confirmed that Drew was a serious competitor, a crowd-pleaser and a potential world-class bronc rider. Most of all, she'd accepted that he wasn't chasing a crazy dream. Through the pressure of competing, traveling, injuries and discovering he had a four-year-old son, Drew was trying his best to be a good father.

Drew Rawlins was twice the man Hallie's father had ever been.

Even though she recognized and respected Drew's talent, the physical strain and danger of the sport posed serious threats to his health. In a short time, he'd become an integral part of Nick's daily existence. Losing Drew to a senseless death would leave a big, black hole in her son's life and Hallie, by herself, would never be able to fill that void.

One minute before seven the phone rang and she jumped, sloshing coffee onto the counter. Pulse pounding, she wondered if she'd imagined the shrill sound. A second jingle confirmed she hadn't. She snatched up the receiver. "Drew?"

"What's wrong? You sound like you're out of breath?"

"I just…you're…" Tears burned her eyes. "Did you win?" Hallie glanced at the calendar, but her blurry eyes couldn't decipher the name of the rodeo he'd competed in today.

"Came in fourth." That meant no prize money. "I slipped out of the standings."

Oh, no. "How far?"

"Sixteen. I'm going for broke at the Texas Stampede in Dallas on the nineteenth and twentieth."

She wished with all her heart that she could convince him to quit the sport, but years from now Nick would hate her if she'd forced his father's hand and cost him a world title.

"Hallie?" Drew's voice interrupted her train of thought.

"I'm here."

"My mom invited us down to her place for Thanksgiving. If you don't already have plans, will you and Nick come?"

Hallie had always spent Thanksgiving with Sharon and several of her single nursing friends. Now, Hallie had no choice but to go where Drew would be, so Nick could spend the holiday with his father and his grand-mother. "Sure, but we'll need to leave on Friday, because I'm scheduled to work that Saturday."

"I'm heading out Friday, too. I'll be bucking in El Paso on Saturday." He cleared his throat. "How are things at the hospital?"

"Fine." The one-word answer escaped her mouth in two syllables, and she cursed the crack in her voice.

"You don't sound fine." The wariness in his voice came through loud and clear. She envisioned Drew clenching his jaw.

Tired of keeping her worries to herself she confessed. "This...this...situation is too hard for Nick." *And me.*

"Where's Nick right now?"

"Playing a video game in his room."

"Go on, I'm listening," he said.

"Nick's whole day revolves around your call." She chose not to mention that she spent much of her day thinking about it also.

"Are you saying you don't want me to phone anymore?"

"I don't know what the answer is, but after watching you ride last week Nick worries about you constantly." She swallowed hard. "A boy Nick's age shouldn't have to worry about his father dying. It's not normal or healthy."

"I'll be there as soon as I can."

"Wait. You don't—"

The line went dead. *Great.* Now she'd have to come up with an excuse as to why Nick didn't get a chance to talk to Drew tonight.

DREW SWUNG THE CAMPER into a parking spot in front of Hallie's apartment and cut the engine. Her panicky voice during the last phone call had prompted a nonstop trip across two states.

God, he was exhausted—thirteen hours of driving and thinking about Hallie, Nick and their impossible situation. Dread seeped into his bones. What if Hallie had reached the end of her rope and he was about to be the recipient of a well-rehearsed "hit the road, Jack" speech?

He left the camper and headed to her apartment, his steps sluggish. At the door he realized he'd left his Stetson on the passenger seat. There was something about a cowboy hat that made a man believe he could face anything and come out the winner. *To hell with the Stetson.* Hallie wasn't sending him packing—at least not tonight. She was the first woman he'd ever considered going the distance for. He'd find a way to make things right.

"Back again, young man?"

"Miss Rose." No escaping the block warden.

"I hear you're Nick's father."

"That's right." Too tired to argue, Drew hoped the old biddy would make her point, then mind her own business.

"You better do right by that boy, you hear? He needs a daddy. You make sure you're a good one."

"Yes, ma'am."

Miss Rose slipped back into her apartment and Drew blew out a breath. He should have expected the news that he was Nick's father to spread like wildfire through the small town.

Hallie's door opened a crack and her eyes peered through the slit. She unlatched the chain, and he entered the apartment. He noticed her trembling fingers when she turned the lock. Eyes welling with tears, she sniffled.

Hold your ground. "Is Nick home?"

"He's at preschool." Her lower lip wobbled. "I took the day off."

Oh, hell. He held out his hand and she threw herself at him, burrowing her cold nose in the crook of his neck. He tightened his hold. For such a small thing, she sure filled his arms.

She smelled like spring—fresh and flowery. He breathed deeply. His hands roamed over her back... her hips...her bottom. Hallie snuggled closer, rubbing against him—not the actions of a woman about to tell a man to get lost.

Exhausted, confused, turned on and frustrated just enough to resist her charms, he said, "I've been worried sick since our call last night." He clasped her face between his hands and rubbed his thumb along her lower lip. "How can I make this easier—"

"Please..." She stood on tiptoe, her mouth inches from his. "We'll talk later."

His stomach clenched. "What about Feller?"

"We're just friends," she said with conviction.

Drew suspected as much but was relieved to hear Hallie admit there was nothing romantic between her and the doctor. For five years she'd haunted his dreams, never allowing him to forget her or what they'd shared that night in his camper. In the back of his mind a voice warned him that taking their relationship to the next level would only complicate their situation. Head dizzy with the taste and scent of her, he struggled to take the high road. "We shouldn't—"

Her mouth swallowed the rest of his sentence. He didn't understand, nor did he care, why she'd chosen this moment to give in to the attraction between them. She grasped his hand and led him down the hallway to her bedroom. He shut the door and flipped the lock.

"Wait," he said when she began unbuttoning her blouse. He went into the master bath, took a shower in record time, then confiscated a new toothbrush from the medicine cabinet. When he stepped from the bathroom, Hallie lay curled on her side in the middle of the bed, wearing nothing but her bra and panties. He fished his wallet from his pants pocket and set it on the nightstand. This time he wouldn't forget to use a condom.

He'd dreamed of this moment and now that it was here, it didn't seem real. He loosened the knotted towel around his waist and the terry cloth dropped to the carpet. Her gaze clung to his when he joined her on the bed.

Eager to reacquaint himself with her body, he cupped her breasts, stroked her stomach, her thighs. He settled his mouth over hers, trying without words to express how much she meant to him—had always meant to him.

Her touches set him on fire, but he refused to rush. He'd take his time. Savor the scent of her skin, the sound of her breathing, the feel of her legs entwined with his. When he finished loving Hallie, there would be no doubt in her mind that he aimed to be her forever cowboy.

Still, reservations teased the edges of his consciousness. Even though he believed this was more than sex, Drew feared when all was said and done Hallie wouldn't need him as badly as he needed her. Little by little, the desperation eased its grip on him, pushed aside by physical need and Hallie's enticing caresses.

Five years ago he'd wanted to erase the sadness from Hallie's eyes. Their lovemaking had left a permanent mark on Drew's soul and the feelings she'd inspired in him that night were demanding to be set free once again. Burying his head between her neck and shoulder, he swallowed hard. Not even the euphoria of winning a rodeo came close to the fiery feelings Hallie inspired in him.

"Hallie, are you sure you…"

"Make love to me, Drew."

"My pleasure, darlin.'"

Slow and easy… Swift and intense… In the aftermath of their union, Drew decided making love to Hallie had been the best thing that could have happened between them.

YOU HAVE NO ONE to blame but yourself.

Making love with Drew was a bad error in judgment on Hallie's part. She should have resisted her attraction to him, but he'd driven straight through the night to get to her. Drew had looked so tired, so defeated standing on her doorstep, that suddenly nothing mattered but being in his arms.

Lately Hallie had felt lonelier than ever. Maybe because Nick didn't shower her with as much affection as he had before Drew entered their lives. Shoving the excuses aside, she admitted that making love had further complicated her and Drew's already difficult relationship.

Drew kissed her forehead. "You okay?"

She didn't trust her voice. Instead, she slid her knee between his thighs and snuggled closer. Obviously, there was a total disconnect between her brain and body. Feeling emotionally gutted, a tear escaped the corner of her eye.

Drew's thumb smeared the drop of moisture across her cheek. "Talk, Hallie. That last phone call scared the hell out of me."

"The preschool bus will drop Nick off in an hour." She refused to discuss anything in her naked state. She needed a barrier between them—preferably clothes. "I imagine you're hungry."

The corner of his mouth tilted. "I'm starving." He rolled off the bed and went into the bathroom, then returned and scooped his jeans off the floor. Conscious of his eyes on her backside, she grabbed her clothes and retreated to the bathroom.

Once they were both dressed, they left the bedroom. She made a pot of coffee and threw together a sandwich for Drew.

"Thanks." He attacked the food.

Hallie added chocolate chip cookies to the meal. "Homemade?" he asked.

"They're Nick's favorite."

"Mine, too." Drew helped himself to a cookie before finishing the rest of the sandwich and pushing the plate away. He leveled a sober stare at Hallie. "I can't make things right until I know what's wrong."

She sat across the table from him. "This isn't working."

"What's not working?"

Even though he never complained about the added stress and pressure of making time for Nick, being super dad and super rodeo cowboy was wearing Drew down. Telling him his effort fell short of the mark bordered on cruelty. "The phone calls and visits aren't enough," she said.

His shoulders stiffened. "I'm doing the best I can."

"Nick needs you." *Because I'm no longer enough.* Yes, she was jealous of Drew and Nick's relationship— she wasn't proud of those feelings, but she owned up to them nonetheless. She'd once been the light of her son's life and feared she'd never have that same closeness with Nick again. "He's picking fights with the kids at school." And with her after school.

Drew's blue eyes turned icy. "And what about you, Hallie? What's your complaint?"

"I'm tired of bearing the brunt of Nick's bad moods when you're not around." She ached for the days when it was just her and Nick and anything she said or did was good enough for her son.

"What are you saying?"

Her heart squeezed painfully inside her chest. "You, me and Nick can't keep this insanity up much longer."

"I'll fit in more visits between now and the end of the month."

A chunk of her heart broke off. Hallie couldn't live with herself if her demands caused Drew to lose his focus. "You're already pushing yourself too hard. Nick just found out he has a father. He'll be devastated if you get injured."

Drew shoved his chair away from the table and paced across the kitchen. Head bowed, he pinched the bridge of his nose between his forefinger and thumb. When he finally faced her, the stark vulnerability in his eyes shocked her.

Hallie feared what she was about to propose wouldn't go over well with Drew or Nick, but in her mind it was the only solution. "I want you to stop visiting and calling."

He clenched his jaw. "You're asking me to ignore my son?"

"Just until after the finals in December." She wanted a chance to reclaim the closeness she'd once felt with Nick and she couldn't do it when Nick's whole world revolved around Drew's phone calls and occasional visits.

The nerve along his jaw pulsed angrily. "I won't walk out on my son."

"It's in Nick's best interest."

Or is it in your best interest? Hallie ignored the voice in her head.

"No," he said.

"No what?"

"No, I won't stop calling or seeing Nick."

"But—"

"This mess is your fault."

She gasped.

"You were the one who chose not to tell me I was a father four years ago, now you have to live with the consequences of your actions."

"I know what's best for my son."

"Our son." Drew continued pacing the width of her kitchen, his brow scrunched in thought. He stopped suddenly and faced her. "I have a solution. You and Nick can join me on the road."

Was he crazy? "I work, Drew. I have a job. Responsibilities at the hospital." Good Lord, being in close quarters with Drew 24/7 would be too enticing. How would they keep their hands off one another? And making love would only weaken Hallie's resolve to keep Drew at a distance—both physically and emotionally. The more they made love, the more her heart would yearn for the three of them to be a real family.

"Traveling together isn't a good idea," she said.

"You don't get to make all the calls, Hallie."

"My job—"

"You must have vacation time coming to you." In three steps, Drew stood before her. "You'll never be able to repay what you took from me and Nick these past four years, but you can start making it up to us by giving us a chance to spend quality time together. Nick will love camping—"

Of course he would, but that wasn't the point. Hallie didn't have a chance to argue, because the front door banged open.

"Mom, is my dad here?"

"We're in the kitchen, honey."

Nick skidded to a stop in the doorway.

"Hey, sport." Drew crossed the room and went down on one knee. "How about a hug?"

When Nick didn't automatically comply, Drew's brow furrowed. He didn't understand their son's up-and-down moods like Hallie did. Nick was happy to see Drew, yet hesitant to show any enthusiasm, because he never knew how long his father would stick around.

Drew clasped Nick's shoulder. "How would you like to travel with me to a bunch of my rodeos?"

Hallie glared at Drew's back.

"Really?" Nick's face lit up with excitement, then he wiggled out of his father's hold and raced across the room. "Can we, Mom? Can we go with Dad? Please?"

Drew's cool gaze dared Hallie to defy him.

Think of the positive side—Nick would have a chance to be with both parents. But the risks were huge—what if Nick loved being with his daddy more than he loved being with his mother? By the end of the road trip would Drew displace Hallie in their son's affections?

Don't you want better for Nick than what you had? Maybe quality time with Nick would convince Drew that his son, not rodeo, deserved to come first in his life.

Feeling as if she were making a monumental mistake, Hallie agreed. "Yes, we can go."

The band of fear around Drew's middle loosened, leaving his insides shaky. He'd narrowly escaped being cut out of Hallie's and Nick's lives. He hated that he'd manipulated the situation, but he'd had no choice. Drew couldn't maintain his current rodeo schedule and keep making pit stops in Bastrop. "Will you have trouble getting time off from work?"

"I've got two weeks vacation coming to me." Hallie offered Nick a cookie, then stowed the container on the pantry shelf.

"And Nick's preschool?"

"Nick's a bright boy." She ruffled his hair. "He'll catch up with the kids when we return."

Drew stared at Hallie. A flicker of longing sparked low in his gut. Traveling together would keep his body in a constant state of arousal. He'd never ridden a bronc with a hard-on and wasn't keen on trying. Even so he couldn't pass up the opportunity to be with his son.

All he had to do was make sure he didn't screw up what might be his only chance to prove to Hallie that rodeo didn't have to interfere with him being a good dad.

Chapter Ten

"When are we gonna be there?"

Oh, bless you, Nick. Hallie had been dying to ask that question for the past twenty miles. She winced when the camper hit a rut in the road. After four hours of sitting on threadbare upholstery stretched over what felt like plywood, the only sensation left in her body was a prickling throb in her backside.

"We got a late start, so we have a ways to go," Drew growled, obviously ticked about their midmorning departure.

In her opinion, ten o'clock was not a late start. Since they'd left the apartment, Nick had been a little whiner. She knew from experience he'd be grumpier if they'd left at 5:00 a.m. as Drew had wanted.

That Drew believed being crammed into a hot tin box on wheels for hours on end promoted family bonding boggled Hallie's mind. She recalled Nick's jubilant expression when Drew had invited them on the road and suspected it was only a matter of time before Nick learned that hanging out with his father wasn't all it was cracked up to be. Selfishly, Hallie hoped Nick would continue to act up, so Drew would become impatient and cut the trip short.

"Why are you staring at me?" The scowl lines across Drew's forehead deepened. "Do I have a booger in my nose?"

Ignoring him, Hallie stretched her legs, her foot bumping a piece of garbage poking from beneath the floor mat—a crumpled fast-food bag.

Hallie liked things in their proper places. Drew liked things wherever they landed. After confiscating a trash bag of food wrappers and paper coffee cups, she determined he ate most of his meals in the driver's seat. Hallie could have used the Handi Wipes in her purse to wash off the half inch of dust and grime covering the cracked dashboard, but with the windows open why bother? At least she had the sense to bring the evergreen air freshener from her car and hang it on the rearview mirror. The spicy pine scent masked the smells of stale leather and greasy food.

"I'm bored," Nick said for the tenth time.

Hallie rummaged through the backpack next to her seat. She'd spent twenty-five dollars at the drug store stocking up on crayons, markers, activity books and action figures. She offered Nick the Star Wars coloring book and a new box of crayons.

"Coloring's for babies." Nick's eyes crossed as he watched himself blow spit bubbles.

If only she'd insisted that they eat lunch inside the restaurant with the children's play area instead of ordering their meals to go. But Drew had wanted to make up time, and she believed the sooner they reached their destination the better for everyone. Now Nick was edgy and restless, because he hadn't had any exercise all day. She wondered how long Drew would hold out before he admitted the road trip hadn't been such a good idea.

She glared at her watch in disbelief. Less than an hour had passed since lunch. "How many miles did you say it is to Fort Stockton?"

"A little over three hundred." He strangled the steering wheel. "If we didn't have to stop every half hour to use a bathroom…"

She swallowed the sarcastic retort on the tip of her tongue. She wasn't the one who'd bought Nick a king-size shake to go with his Happy Meal.

"Hey, Dad?"

"What?"

"How long 'til we get there?"

"It's going to be a while, Nick."

"Mom?"

"What, honey?"

"How long's a while?"

"Four or five *Captain Earth* episodes."

"Oh, man!"

Hallie went back to staring out the window. The scenery had long ago lost its appeal. A person could only stare at wide bottomlands and grassy plains for so long before everything blurred into one big lump of boring beige.

Drew pointed out the windshield. "There's a turnoff ahead."

Squinting against the sun's glare, she searched the horizon for an exit, but didn't see one. "You said this highway takes us straight into Stockton."

"It does. But I remember using a shortcut a few years back. Saved me almost an hour."

He slowed the camper, then moved onto the shoulder. The road—if you could call it that—was a narrow strip of rutted dirt, sand and rock.

Clutching the armrest, Hallie braced herself, as Drew turned onto the path. Brush and plants grew almost to the middle of the road. "I think we should turn back."

"Jeez, Hallie, settle down. You'll worry Nick."

A glance over her shoulder confirmed that their son was anything but concerned. As the camper dipped and thunked along the uneven ground, Nick's grin widened.

They'd traveled a short distance when suddenly the back end of the camper dropped. Drew hit the brakes and Hallie clutched the dashboard as the camper rocked to a standstill.

"Whoa, that was cool, Dad."

Angry, Hallie snapped at Drew. "I warned you not to take the shortcut."

"If we'd left this morning when I'd wanted to we'd have arrived in Fort Stockton three hours ago."

She pointed her finger. "Don't blame this on me. You're the one who left the highway."

He glared at her finger, then opened the driver-side door and dropped out of sight—literally. Before Hallie's mind registered what had happened, a loud grunt and curses filled the air.

"Drew?" She unhooked her seat belt and scrambled onto the driver's seat. Cautiously she peered out the door. Drew lay motionless at the bottom of the ravine. Good Lord, had he struck his head?

"Nick, stay here." Her heart racing, Hallie eased out of the camper, planting her feet on the six inches of packed dirt between the tires and the edge of the road. "Drew!"

"I'm fine." He sounded winded.

Frantic to reach his side, she ignored the prickly weeds scratching her arms and hands as she descended into the ditch. "Don't move." She tested a large rock below her right foot, then climbed down a few more feet before jumping to the bottom. Her boots landed inches from Drew's head, spewing dust in his face.

Eyes closed, he coughed and wheezed. He'd torn his jeans, bloodied his knee and scraped his palms from grabbing hold of the rocks to slow his fall.

"Where does it hurt the most?" She examined his head and neck.

"Do you really care?"

If only you knew how much, cowboy. "I care. You're the only one who can drive that stupid camper." She ignored his rude snort and smoothed her hands along his thighs and calves. "Your legs aren't broken. Did you sprain an ankle?"

"Ankles are fine. But I hurt here." His mouth tightened when he touched his stomach.

They were in big trouble if Drew had broken his ribs or suffered an internal injury. She didn't have the strength to drag his carcass out of the ditch, and she didn't dare leave him alone in the middle of nowhere while she went for help. Blast it! She should have never agreed to this trip.

Hallie tugged Drew's shirt from the waistband of his jeans and slid her hands beneath the material. Gingerly she pressed her fingertips against the rock-hard muscle beneath his rib cage. "Tell me when you feel pain."

"There." She moved her fingers. "There, too," he said, his eyes suspiciously bright.

As Hallie's fingers edged lower across his abdomen, Drew's breathing grew labored. "Did the buckle gouge you?"

"I don't know."

She pressed the area below his hipbone.

"Oh, man."

Hallie couldn't find any evidence of an injury. "Show me where it pains you the most."

"Right here." He placed her hand over his fly.

Shock immobilized her. Her heart was pounding with fear and he teased her? She'd tried to be patient with Drew today, sensing his need to adjust to her and Nick's presence. If persuaded, she might even forgive his male bullheadedness in taking the disastrous shortcut. But no way would she put up with cutesy sex games. "You mean this?" She squeezed the stiff appendage.

"Yeeeoww!" Drew scrambled to his feet, knocking Hallie on her rump.

When she stood, her boots slid, and she crashed into a prickly weed. Plant spikes poked through her clothes, fueling her anger.

Bent at the waist, Drew cupped his crotch. "That was downright mean."

"You ain't seen mean yet, cowboy."

"Hey, Dad! I gotta go, too!" Nick leaned out the camper door and pointed to the front of his pants.

"Get away from that door, young man!" The last thing she needed was for Nick to injure himself.

"I gotta pee."

Hallie clawed her way up the side of the ravine. Drew followed, his hot breath caressing her neck. When her foot slipped, he pressed his body to hers, preventing her from sliding to the bottom. A searing heat scorched her spine, but she ignored it. Regaining her footing, she forged ahead.

When they reached the top of the ravine, Drew limped around the camper to the passenger door. "Hop out on this side." Nick followed Drew to the back end of the camper.

Fuming, Hallie sat on the front fender, tapping her sneaker against the ground. She waited a full minute before checking on father and son. The grave look on Drew's face sent Hallie's stomach into a nosedive. Both back tires were flat.

Drew rubbed his brow. "There's only one spare."

And to think she worried about Nick having a chance to stretch his legs. By the end of the day their legs would be stretched all the way to Fort Stockton.

"If I replace one tire, we can limp back to the highway," Drew said.

"Turn around?" The road was barely wider than the camper. "Are you crazy?" She snorted. "Don't answer that."

He stepped closer, his breath hitting her square in the face. "I can't think with you making noises like a puffed-up green bronc on a cold morning."

She had no idea what a puffed-up green bronc was and didn't care.

"Mom."

Ignoring Nick, she said, "Your stubbornness got us into this mess."

"Dad."

"Settle down, would you?" Drew shoved a hand through his hair.

"Mom. Dad."

"What!" Hallie and Drew shouted in unison.

Nick handed Hallie the cell phone from her purse. "You said to call 911 if I ever got in trouble."

BARELY ELEVEN in the morning and already campers were firing up the barbecues for lunch. The smell of lighter fluid hung heavy in the air, and it wouldn't be long before a thick, smoky haze covered the campsite.

Drew sat in a lawn chair, watching Nick kick a soccer ball around the campground with a freckle-faced boy twice his age. Drew had offered to play with Nick while Hallie showered, but his son had chosen a stranger over his father. Hallie hadn't spoken more than a few sentences to Drew since yesterday's fiasco. He didn't blame her. The road was no place for a kid.

If only he hadn't panicked when Hallie had wanted to cut him out of her and Nick's life until after the finals in December. She'd left him with no choice but to suggest traveling together. His relationship with Nick was tenuous at best and he feared a long separation would alienate his son even more.

Recalling the danger he'd put Hallie and Nick in yesterday twisted his gut. If he hadn't been so peeved about their late start, he'd have never taken the shortcut. During the three hours they'd waited for a tow, he'd had plenty of time to mull things over. He'd admitted that

Hallie's presence shot his concentration to heck and back. He'd been positive he could handle his attraction to her, but he hadn't counted on Hallie destroying every shred of common sense he possessed.

A shudder passed through him when he acknowledged how poorly he'd ridden lately. He had to win big in Dallas. Even then, Fitzgerald and the cowboys ahead of him in the standings would have to suffer a run of bad luck in Vegas for Drew to have a shot at the title.

Closing his eyes, he practiced drawing in deep breaths, trying to ignore the ache. He didn't dare tell Hallie he'd bruised his ribs when he'd fallen into the ravine. She'd nag him to get an X-ray and spending hours in an E.R. waiting room would bore Nick.

"Kenny's gotta go to his grandma's," Nick said, sneaking up behind Drew. "There's nothing to do."

Drew was discovering that four-year-old boys needed constant physical activity. "Want me to kick the ball around with you?"

Nick shrugged. At least he hadn't come right out and said no. "When's Mom gonna be done?" Nick stared in the direction of the campground showers.

"How long does it take your mother to shower and dress?"

Another shrug.

Drew reached out to ruffle the mop of sweaty hair, but Nick moved his head out of the way. Tamping down the hurt at his son's action, Drew asked, "Are you looking forward to the rodeo tonight?"

Silence. Nick's cold shoulder chipped away at Drew's confidence.

"Dad?"

"Yeah."

Nick finally looked Drew in the eye. "Are you mad at Mom?"

"Why do you ask?"

"She said she shoulda tried harder to find you."

Nick's words caught Drew off-guard. He reflected on all the moments he'd missed out on with his son. Yet, each time Nick called him *Dad* some of the anger dissipated. He'd been called *Dad* often enough these past weeks that he had to dig deep to find any resentment. "I'm more sad than mad."

"How come?"

"I'm sad I wasn't there when you lost your first tooth."

Nick scowled. "You woulda grounded me."

"For losing a tooth?"

"I walked in front of the swings at the park and a girl kicked me in the mouth."

"Ouch. That must have hurt."

"Mom got mad 'cause she told me to go behind the swings."

Drew chuckled. No matter what the future held for him and Hallie, he'd never regret the past. Hallie had given him Nick, and his son was by far the best gift he'd ever received. Somehow Drew would find a way to be there for Nick in every way that mattered.

After a long silence, Nick asked, "Are you gonna be my dad forever?"

"Yep. You couldn't get rid of me even if you wanted to." Drew pulled Nick close for a hug, ignoring the way he stiffened. Being a father and a rodeo cowboy at the same time was about as easy as riding a bronc backward.

Most nights he went to bed feeling as if he'd been bucked off before the buzzer.

After a few seconds, Nick relaxed and wrapped his skinny arms around Drew's neck and squeezed. At that moment, with Nick's warm body snuggled close, Drew forgot about his rodeo goals. "What do you and your mom do for fun?"

"Sometimes we go to the park."

There was no kiddie park in the campground.

"Once we went to the ocean."

There were no oceans nearby.

"Mostly I play with my friends 'cause Mom's gotta work."

Funny how Drew had believed he'd been the one cheated out of time with his son all these years. But in order to support them, Hallie had to work, which meant she missed out on spending time with Nick, too.

"As soon as your mom's ready, we'll head into town before the rodeo and do something fun."

"Can we go putt-putt?"

"You mean miniature golf?"

Nick's head bobbed up and down.

"Sure."

"Cool. I'm gonna play soccer by myself." Nick kicked the ball out from under Drew's chair and took off toward the grassy patch nearby.

A few moments later Hallie's voice floated into Drew's ear. "I'm ready."

Drew glanced sideways and nearly tipped the chair over. *Wow.* He gaped at her silky smooth thighs. The tight denim skirt, studded silver belt buckle and red leather boots made her legs appear twice as long. Forcing his gaze higher, he noted the top half of Hallie was as sexy as the bottom half. When she shifted from one boot to the other, her red bandana print blouse pulled tight across her breasts. *Double wow.*

She'd styled her hair different. The strands flowed like a smooth blond waterfall down the middle of her back. He curled his hands into fists to keep from reaching for the silky mass, knowing from experience her hair felt as velvety as it looked.

"Ah…" He couldn't remember if she'd asked him a question.

Her mouth curved into a knowing smile.

Just then a car horn blared, jarring him out of his stupor. "What did you say?"

She stepped closer, and he caught a whiff of perfume. "Where's Nick?"

"Kicking the ball around."

Their eyes met and held. He braced himself, wondering if there would ever come a time when a heated look from Hallie wouldn't knock him off balance.

She fidgeted with the hem of her skirt. "I know you're trying to do what's best for Nick, but—"

Fearing Hallie was on the verge of asking him to take her and Nick back to Bastrop, Drew slipped his arm around her hip and coaxed her to stand between his thighs. He cupped her face, bringing it closer to his. When her pink tongue licked the corner of her mouth he was lost.

The kiss was short and hard—her response, bold and sure. He wanted the kiss to lead to more, but this wasn't the place or time. Drew grinned. "Nice boots."

She twirled in front of him. "So you like the outfit?"

Like it? "God, Hallie, you're killing me in that miniskirt." He caressed her thigh, and she swatted playfully at his hand. "I promised to take Nick into town for a round of miniature golf before we head over to the rodeo."

Right then Nick returned with the soccer ball. "Dad said we're gonna go play putt-putt."

"I heard." Hallie hated miniature golf.

A half hour later she silently fumed as she stood by and waited for Drew to pay for their rounds of golf at Billy Bob's Miniature Golfland. So far the day hadn't gone as she'd hoped. Nick had been angry with Drew when he'd woken this morning and Hallie expected Drew to raise the white flag and suggest they return to Bastrop. Instead, he'd gone out of his way to show Nick a good time.

"Here, Mom." Nick handed her a putter and a pink golf ball, then turned to Drew. "Mom hates putt-putt." So the secret was out—yes, she hated the stupid game and because of that she rarely took Nick to play at the course in Bastrop.

"Really?" Drew grinned. "I love putt-putt."

Of course Drew would find a way to get back on his son's good side. She followed the pair to the first hole and putted. Missed the hole by a mile.

"Watch this," Nick said. He glanced at Drew—not her—to make sure his father was watching.

"Good try, Nick." Drew swung his club. "Looks like you have the best position."

Her son beamed at Drew. Hallie was all but forgotten

as they made their way through the course. Neither Nick nor Drew noticed the one hole she made par on. For all intents and purposes, she was invisible.

When they finished, they returned the putters to the clubhouse and Drew tallied up the scores. "Nick won."

"Cool!" Nick looked at Hallie. "I bet Mom came in last place."

"She did." Drew chuckled. "Maybe a root beer at the stand down the street would cheer your mom up."

The last thing Hallie needed was cheering up.

"Wanna root beer, Mom?" Nick asked.

Pasting a smile on her face she said, "As a matter of fact, I do." She expected Nick to take her hand as they walked back to the camper but he reached for Drew's. Ignoring the achy feeling building in her throat, Hallie trudged behind the males, hating that she'd lost ground in the competition to keep the number-one spot in her son's heart.

Chapter Eleven

Hallie spotted her snoozing son. Nick was curled up in an old quilt, lying a few feet from where Drew sat on a rock and fished. Nick's head rested near Ted, the terry-cloth bear Sharon had given him for his first birthday. The stuffed animal's arms and legs protruded at awkward angles—the result of the numerous surgeries to reattach severed limbs. The nap would do Nick good—eight hours of sleep a night wasn't enough for an active boy his age.

She wanted to resent Drew—it was his crazy rodeo schedule that prevented Nick from getting proper rest. But how could she, when Nick was having the time of his life? Her once petulant, argumentative, stubborn son had morphed into a sweet, fun-loving child since the miniature golf game six days ago. It wasn't fair that Drew did one activity with Nick and suddenly their son forgave him for being absent most of his life.

Forcing her thoughts in a different direction, she scanned the campground. As far as parks went, this one was nothing to brag about—flat, dusty terrain with scraggly trees. At least the small lake had been stocked with catfish. Nick had caught two yesterday.

Drew stretched an arm above his head, then both shoulders hunched. His relaxed posture didn't fool her. He'd been edgy and restless since waking this morning. The rodeo outside Fort Stockton hadn't gone well. He'd come in second. To add to his troubles he'd phoned Brody for an update on the competition and heard he'd slipped to seventeenth in the standings.

Hallie didn't understand much about rodeo except that it all came down to money. The fifteen cowboys with the highest earnings at the end of the season competed in Vegas. The maximum rodeos a cowboy could count toward their earnings in one season was seventy, and Drew had hit sixty this past week. No wonder his body was always bruised and battered—there was no time to heal between competitions. Hallie didn't ask about Drew's earnings and he hadn't volunteered the information, but she suspected if he didn't win the Texas Stampede in Dallas his run for the title would end.

If only she hadn't caved in and made love with Drew. The experience had connected her to him on an emotional level. Half of her wanted to see him succeed at being a good father not only for Nick, but also for himself. She honestly appreciated Drew's determination to take his role as father to Nick seriously, but part of her resented going from being *everything* to Nick to being *some* things to him.

"How long has he been asleep?" she whispered, sneaking up behind Drew.

Switching the fishing pole to his right hand, Drew said, "He conked out a half hour ago." Drew's eyes remained transfixed on the bobber floating in the water—

as if his intense mental concentration would provoke the next catfish that swam by to catch itself on the hook.

"That's cheating, you know," she said. Father and son had made a wager on who would reel in the biggest prize before they packed up and headed to Dallas.

"What's cheating?"

"Fishing while Nick's asleep," she said.

"No four-year-old's going to show me up."

For the umpteenth time, she noticed Drew's hair needed a trim. Silky black strands brushed his shirt collar and covered his ears. He looked like a bad boy who rode Harleys, not horses. "You're awfully quiet."

"Thinking about my ride in Dallas."

Drew always contemplated the future—the next rodeo, campground or fast food restaurant. "Don't you ever stop to smell the proverbial roses?"

"I'm enjoying the here and now." His testy response claimed otherwise. He rolled his shoulders and tilted his neck from side to side.

She moved behind him and massaged his back. "Sore?"

One eyebrow lifted. "A kink. It'll work itself out."

He blew off her concern all the time and it hurt, because she truly cared about his well-being. Arguing about his health did no good, so she kept quiet and lightly probed his muscles. When she pressed against his collarbone he stiffened—another bruise. He was pushing his luck.

At the rodeo in Fort Stockton she'd heard whispers. Cowboys and fans had commented on Drew's age. She gathered most competitors retired from the sport by the time they reached thirty. At thirty-two, Drew was considered old.

"How do your ribs feel?" she asked, knowing he wouldn't tell her the truth.

"Fine." Drew was fine even when he wasn't. He dropped his head forward and groaned when her fingers inched down his spine. "What was it like?" he asked.

"What was what like?"

"Giving birth to Nick."

An overwhelming sadness filled her, almost suffocating in its intensity. She remembered thinking of Drew and wondering where he was while she'd labored to bring their son into the world. "Giving birth to Nick was the scariest, most wonderful experience of my life."

He leaned against her and closed his eyes. "When was he born?"

"May fifteenth. He was a week overdue." She ran her fingers through Drew's hair—it was similar in weight and texture to Nick's. "My water broke during one of my nursing clinicals." She smiled at the memory of her panicked classmates arguing with one another over how to handle the situation. "Sharon was my instructor at the time, and she stayed with me until Nick was born."

Drew set the fishing pole on the ground, then grasped her hand and pulled her around in front of him. "I bet you thought of your foster mother that day."

Drew's sensitive understanding warmed Hallie's heart. "I did."

"You said she died before Nick was born."

"Margaret suffered a stroke and died the day I stitched your head in the E.R. five years ago." How much easier her life would have been had her foster mother lived to help Hallie raise her son. "I wish she could have seen Nick."

"No wonder you looked so sad that night I ran into you at Cozie's."

Hallie nodded. "It hit me pretty hard that I was totally alone in the world. My friends were trying to cheer me up."

"Then you found out you were pregnant and—"

"And that's what kept me going. My child needed me and I was determined to be there for him, so I snapped out of my funk."

"How long were you in labor?" Drew asked.

"Twelve hours." The doctor almost performed a C-section because Nick was so big.

"How much did he weigh?"

"Eight pounds twelve ounces."

Drew rested his hands against her stomach, splaying his fingers from hip-to-hip. She smiled at the awe on his face. "It wasn't easy, believe me."

Their eyes met and held, then he swayed forward, his mouth touching her forehead, her eyelids, her cheek and by the time he set his cool lips on hers, a hot, achy knot had formed in her belly.

Drew was the only man capable of triggering such an intense need in her body. The charged awareness between them was too difficult to fight, explain or deny—it just was and always would be.

He ended the kiss. "We're getting a motel in Dallas," he said.

She understood the risks that came with making love a second time and they were real and frightening. As Nick's father Drew had already carved a place for himself in her heart. If she wasn't careful, by the end of the road trip he'd hold the organ in the palm of his hand, leaving her with nothing but memories and a gaping hole in her chest.

"I want you bad, Hallie." The muscle along Drew's jaw flexed. "We're good together." He nibbled a path down her neck, destroying her defenses.

Tell me you love me, Drew.

He wouldn't. Because even if he did care for her deeply, the only thing Drew loved was rodeo.

"Say, yes." He nuzzled her mouth.

Her mind insisted there could be no future with a man who might be alive one moment and dead the next—by choice. But her heart refused to give up on Drew. She had to find a way to make him care more about her and Nick than his damned rodeo.

"Yes, we'll get a motel room in Dallas." She'd deal with the consequences later.

Before things got out of hand and Nick woke, Drew reached for the fishing pole. Struggling to bring his body under control, he walked a few feet away and recast the line.

Darn Hallie. He'd tried to keep his distance, but the more he pushed her away, the more he wanted her.

The more he needed her.

She messed up his thoughts so badly that he'd begun to question his riding instincts—the pains in his body testified to that. Nothing posed a greater threat to a cowboy than a lack of focus. Before each ride, he'd conjure up a picture of himself taming a wild bronc. Lately all he got for the effort was a pathetic image of himself astride an old bag of bones ready for the glue factory.

Last night when he lay in the dark he'd pondered retiring, but he couldn't accept the idea of hanging up his spurs when he had a chance to win the big one. He wanted to be the kind of man his son could look up to and be proud of. If he walked away from rodeo now, one day Nick would judge that decision and Drew didn't want his son believing him a coward.

Hallie joined him at the edge of the lake. He felt the pull in her soft brown eyes. He'd never been comfortable talking about personal matters, but Hallie made him want to open up to her. "I've been thinking about the past."

"Recent past or long-ago past?"

It had been a while since he'd spoken to anyone about his childhood. "I joined the rodeo circuit to impress my father. The first time I went flying over a bronc's head, I almost quit." He remembered the pain of a tailbone too sore to sit on for a week.

"Dad laughed and said I'd never make it to the big time. I intended to prove him wrong and kept riding. I got better." He blinked rapidly, trying to dispel the hazy image of his angry father threatening to kick him out of the house if he didn't quit wasting money on entry fees. "After I graduated from high school I hit the road and didn't look back."

He'd kept in touch with his mother and had even managed to return home for a holiday or two each year, but the tension between him and his father had kept the visits short. "When my father was diagnosed with cancer and given a few months to live I decided it was time to bury the hatchet." Drew clenched his hand into a fist when he recalled the way things had ended between them. "My father buried the hatchet all right—in my head."

"What happened?"

"Let's just say he didn't change his opinion of me or rodeo." Drew gave in to the need to hold Hallie. He tucked her against his side and buried his nose in her hair. Not until she and Nick had come into his life had he ever questioned his desire to keep riding. Acknowledging his fears and uncertainties didn't come easy for a man like him.

Lately he'd suffered from nightmares—scenes of being hauled out of the arena on a stretcher, and Hallie and Nick turning their backs on him and walking away. Not even the dread of his own mortality disturbed him as much as not having Hallie and Nick in his life.

He released Hallie, then picked up a small rock from the ground. He skimmed the stone across the water's surface, counting three skips before the pebble vanished from sight. Was there a parallel between his life and the stone? Had he managed to go through each day only skimming the surface? How many more chances would he get before the water grabbed him and sucked him under one final time?

He knew he couldn't rodeo forever—that's why he'd purchased Dry Creek Acres. But right now he didn't want to stop bustin' broncs. Not yet. Not when his dream was within reach.

He thought of the years he'd invested in the sport. He'd sacrificed his blood, soul and pride to get a second chance at making it to the NFR. Selfishly, he wanted to push his body to the limit. He craved to find out what he was made of. To prove his old man wrong and amount to *something*.

"Drew?" Hallie nudged him with her elbow.

"Huh?"

"What happens if you don't make the finals in December?"

"I don't know." If he fell short again, Drew wasn't sure he could call it quits for good.

The warmth drained from Hallie's eyes, leaving them the color of muddy lake water. "Tell me one thing," she said. "Is the fame and glory worth the risk?"

Drew stared at Nick asleep on the ground. "God, I hope so."

Two o'clock in the morning.

A bead of sweat slid down Drew's temple as he rested next to Nick on the motel bed, the constant hum of the air conditioner reverberating through his head like a badly tuned banjo.

Since they'd arrived in Dallas three days ago a feeling of desperation had steadily built in Drew. He'd managed to slip away from Hallie and Nick for a few hours when they'd first arrived in the city and had met up with Brody at the American Airlines Center. Brody had filled him in on the gossip behind the chutes. Riley Fitzgerald had been spouting his big mouth off, claiming Drew had peaked earlier in the season and predicted he wouldn't make the cut for the NFR. Most of his competitors had concurred that Drew's days as a premier bronc rider were numbered. The cowboys had only voiced what Drew had feared for weeks—he was washed up.

Drew had quieted the naysayers when he'd pulled

down the top score in his first two rides. The announcers had nicknamed him the dark horse. And Drew didn't mind admitting he'd been mighty pleased when Fitzgerald had gotten bucked off yesterday. Drew didn't feel a bit sorry for the guy. Fitzgerald had already made enough money this season to guarantee himself a spot in Vegas next month.

Drew's anxiety level went up a notch when he pictured the bronc he'd drawn for today's competition— Gut Twister. The same damned horse that had thrown Fitzgerald. Drew could no longer ignore the voice in his head that insisted Hallie and Nick had to leave town before he rode. If he was going to lose his chance at a world title he didn't want to blame anyone but himself.

Eyes burning from lack of sleep, he rested his forearm across his brow. Hallie's image formed in his mind. The woman was like a drug, her smell and taste addictive. Knowing he'd do anything to get close to her scared the bejeezus out of him. Even now, his bruised, battered and exhausted body tightened with lust when he thought of all the places he yearned to touch her.

So bad was his need for Hallie, that as soon as Nick had drifted off to sleep last night he'd coaxed her into the bathroom. He'd found ways to make love in the small cubicle that were ingenious. Like the broncs he rode, their lovemaking had been fierce and wild. And she'd matched his eagerness touch for touch, kiss for kiss, until they'd both gone down in flames.

Afterward there hadn't been time for any tender talk—not with Nick sleeping in the same room. With no demands or promises, they'd retired to separate beds and he'd fallen into an exhausted slumber.

Hours ago, after Nick had drifted off to sleep, he'd done the first smart thing all week—he'd ignored the blatant sexual desire in Hallie's eyes. Brushing aside her caresses, he'd complained of a headache. His plan had backfired. She'd touched his forehead and rubbed his temples. Finally, he'd pushed her hands away and had gone outside to cool off by the motel pool.

When he'd returned to the room, Hallie had been reading a magazine in bed. Her eyes had pleaded for an explanation, but talking would have led to touching and another rendezvous in the bathroom, so he'd crawled into bed with Nick and rolled his back to her.

"You might as well get whatever it is that's bothering you off your chest."

Startled by Hallie's sleep-slurred words, Drew lifted his arm from his forehead. He stared at the shadowy outline of her body on the bed across from him. Her eyes were closed, her breathing even. He wouldn't be surprised if he'd imagined her voice. Heck, the past few weeks he'd questioned his own sanity.

"Have I upset you?" she whispered.

He stared at the mass of tangled blond hair spread across her pillow and wished he didn't feel this desperate need to have her near him. She'd never understand the reason he had to send her away. "Don't worry. Go back to sleep."

"You haven't touched me all day, Drew. You won't even look me in the eye." She fussed with the pillows, then sat up and switched on the bedside lamp. "We can handle this one of two ways. You tell me what's wrong, or I pester you with questions until you give in."

Sassy woman. He wondered where to begin. Her solemn stare suggested he cut to the chase. He'd keep things simple and begin at the end. "I want you to rent a car and leave for Bastrop before I ride today."

Silence greeted his announcement. Hoping to reassure her, he said, "My asking you guys to leave has nothing to do with you or—"

"Your reason has everything to do with me, if you don't want me here." She crushed the extra pillow on the bed to her chest.

He swung his legs to the floor and sat up. Resting his head in his hands, he scrunched his toes against the scratchy carpet. "I don't know how else to say this, Hallie, but straight out. You're too much of a distraction." He crawled onto her bed and pulled her into his arms. Instantly, the warmth of her body broke the tension in him.

This was the dangerous part. She made him forget the important things—like rodeo and winning. He kissed the top of her head. "I lose my bearings when you're around."

"But I never disturb you when you're getting ready to ride. I don't talk. I don't give you advice. I've even kept my mouth shut when you fall on your butt."

He chuckled. "I know, darlin'. It's nothing you've done."

Her hand caressed his bare chest. "Then why do Nick and I have to go?"

"One look from you is all it takes to rattle my brain."

"How can you see me behind the chutes?"

Her mouth was too near to ignore and he dipped his head for a kiss. This past week, there hadn't been time for soft touches or caresses. He almost enjoyed the tender kisses as much as the down and dirty stuff. *Almost.*

He nibbled her lower lip until she opened wide, then slid his tongue inside and searched the damp softness. "Usually I don't waste time contemplating things to death, but I've thought a lot about you and me." He thumped his chest with his fist. "I feel it here. We're right. We're good."

"Then why are you pushing me away?" Her brown eyes glittered with emotion.

He eased out of her arms. "I need to keep you and Nick separate from rodeo. Before I move on with my life, make any new commitments, I have to finish the season." He studied Nick huddled in a ball beneath the blankets. Drew's throat tightened when he recalled all the good times they'd shared during the trip. They'd become as close as any father and son who'd known each other all their lives.

Hallie launched herself at his back, her lush breasts pressing into him. She kissed a path up his neck. "Nick will be disappointed."

He bit the inside of his cheek until he tasted blood. "He'll get over it. Besides, we'll be together at Thanksgiving."

Hallie backed away from him and the loss of her warmth caused his skin to break out in bumps. Frustrated, he whispered loudly, "I don't know what else to do, Hallie. If I don't win tomorrow, then Vegas is out and I'll have to start over again next year."

The softness in Hallie's eyes faded, replaced by a cold glare. "You almost had me fooled, believing you're nothing like my father."

He didn't appreciate being compared to her father, but he refrained from arguing. He'd busted his hump the past few months trying to prove himself to Hallie. Evidently, she'd settle for nothing less than his soul. Well, damn it. He wasn't ready to part with his soul— not yet.

"I don't understand cowboys at all. How can a woman compete with bulls or broncs?"

"I'm not going anywhere, Hallie. I intend to be a part of your and Nick's future." He clenched his hands. "But I need to do this my way."

"If you lose in Vegas, you expect me and Nick to put up with another year of hit-or-miss visits?" Fire spit from her eyes, warning him that he'd gone about this all wrong.

He hadn't planned on using the topic of marriage to persuade Hallie to leave. But desperate men did desperate things. "You're twisting my words. I want to marry you, Hallie."

Chapter Twelve

I want to marry you.

Hallie stared at Drew in shock. Where were the words *I love you?* She squelched the urge to react until she deciphered his true intentions.

"Not quite the proposal every woman dreams of." He pressed her palm against his chest, his thundering heartbeat giving her hope that he'd confess his feelings for her.

"Took about thirty seconds and the first sight of your smile, before my saddle slipped." He tucked a strand of loose hair behind her ear, caressing her skin with his fingertip. "All I'm asking for is a little time—time to see this thing through in Vegas. After the rodeo we'll get married."

What about love? Did he even care if *she* loved him? And if two people loved each other shouldn't they have equal say in things—especially marriage? Testing the waters, she asked, "If you get hurt today will you promise not to compete in Vegas?"

For a long moment he stared at her, his eyes stark with fear, his expression tormented. He exhaled slowly. "If I can't ride, I'll quit. You have my word."

Hallie gathered his promise close to her heart. That Drew was willing to put her and Nick ahead of his quest for a title freed the love she'd felt for Drew these past weeks but had refused to acknowledge for fear he'd take advantage of her. "Okay." The word escaped her mouth on a shaky sigh.

"Okay, what?"

"Nick and I will leave for Bastrop after he wakes up."

The corner of his mouth curved upward. "And the marrying part?"

Her heart urged her to say yes to Drew's proposal. Her head begged caution, warning her not to rush into a commitment that might lead to heartache. And a third voice insisted her son deserved a real family. Marrying Drew would go a long way in making amends to Nick for not allowing his father to be a part of his life from the very beginning.

You're going to marry him out of a sense of guilt?

No. I love him. Hallie loved Drew. Now, she needed to hear those same words from Drew. "Yes."

Drew grinned. "Yes, you'll marry me?"

She nodded. *Tell me you love me. Reassure me that I'm not making a mistake.*

Drew tightened his arms around her. Tiny electric pulses crackled where their skin rubbed. Feeling reckless, she shoved her worries to the back of her mind and gave herself over to the moment.

His tongue slid between her lips and a groan rumbled in his throat as he caressed her breast. "Nick," she whispered, vaguely aware of the need to be quiet.

Drew led her by the hand into the dark bathroom,

locking them inside. He backed her against the door, then tugged her T-shirt over her head. She wanted to touch him, memorize the feel of his perspiration-slick skin, the smooth planes of his chest and the taut muscles in his arms. When she hugged his waist, a sharp breath escaped his mouth. "Tender?"

"Pulled muscle," he said.

Hallie had caught a glimpse of Drew changing clothes before bed and had noticed the black and blue marks on his torso. Yesterday he'd been thrown into the rails during his dismount after the buzzer.

Drew kissed a path down her neck and across her collarbone. A sense of urgency built in her and she pressed herself against him. His briefs hit the floor, then he fumbled inside his shaving kit for protection. He lifted her against him. "I need you."

Their lovemaking was raw and primal and, for Hallie, bittersweet as she waited for that allusive confession of love. The end came swiftly and without warning for both. As the tremors died down, and their bodies cooled, Drew rubbed his callused hand over her back. How could a man used to taming wild broncs hold her with such tenderness?

The last vestiges of passion faded, leaving behind lingering doubts and uncertainties. Hallie buried her face in the crook of his neck and prayed for the strength to resist asking Drew to scratch today's ride and return to Bastrop with her and Nick. Drew promised her a future—on his terms. She wanted their future to begin here and now. Not later. Not after his ride today. Not after Vegas.

"I'll call a rental company and arrange for a car to be delivered to the motel."

Her eyes watered. "That's fine."

"I can make you happy, Hallie. All I need is a little time. After Vegas, we'll be a real family." Drew flipped on the light, then turned on the shower. "Everything's going to be okay, you'll see."

To Hallie's way of thinking they were a long way from being okay.

"WHERE'S DAD?"

Hallie zipped her makeup bag closed. "He's in the lobby checking us out."

Nick grabbed the remote off the nightstand and pointed it at the TV. Plopping down on the end of the bed, he stuffed his teddy bear under his arm and sullenly watched cartoons.

She held her breath. When Nick didn't erupt into a tantrum, the air seeped from her lungs, leaving her light-headed. Or maybe she was woozy because she'd lost her equilibrium after agreeing to marry Drew.

A mere six hours ago, she and Drew had made love. They'd whispered promises, shared heated kisses and burning touches. A part of her had hoped he'd change his mind and beg her to stay. But his offer to call the rental-car company had stung like a nasty wasp bite. After they'd awoken, Drew had gone on a doughnut run, but she'd lost her appetite sometime in the middle of the night between his "Marry me," and her "Okay, Nick and I will return to Bastrop."

While Drew was out she'd broken the news to Nick. First, he'd begged and whined, wanting to remain with

Drew. Then, he'd cried. Then silence. And finally, dark looks that blamed everything on her.

Wanting to cry herself, she shoved her seesawing emotions aside, determined to keep her composure and make their departure as painless as possible.

The shrill ring of the room phone startled her. "Hello?"

"It's Brody. Drew's not picking up his cell. Is he there with you?"

"He's checking us out of the motel."

"Tell him his ride's been moved up to noon. Hector Gomez withdrew because of an injury."

Hallie glanced at the clock on the nightstand. Ten-thirty. Now their goodbyes would be rushed. "Okay. I'll let him know."

"Thanks."

"You're welcome." She waited for Brody to end the call, but he didn't.

"Did Drew tell you about the horse he got stuck with?"

The odd note in the bull rider's voice triggered a creepy sensation along her spine. "No."

"Gut Twister. Orneriest son of a bi— Gun." He cleared his throat. "How's Drew acting? Is he nervous?"

She didn't answer right away, distracted by the images of evil geldings with nasty names running through her mind.

"Hallie?"

"Sorry. Drew seems fine."

"Good. Are you coming to the rodeo?"

"No. Nick and I are leaving for Bastrop before Drew's ride."

"Generous of you to give Drew some breathing room." A note of grudging respect echoed in the cowboy's voice. Too bad the return trip to Bastrop hadn't been her idea.

"Tell Drew I'll wait for him in the cowboy-ready area."

"Sure."

"Hallie…"

"Yes?"

"Drive safe."

The gentle words surprised her. "I will."

The line went dead. As she hung up the phone, Drew entered the room. He paused in the doorway, his Stetson tilted low over his tanned face. Wisps of black hair brushed his shirt collar.

Drew's expression remained blank, reflecting none of the turmoil inside her. When he noticed the luggage on the bed, his lips pressed into a thin line. Maybe her and Nick's leaving bothered him more than he let on. Sadly, that didn't make her feel better.

Returning to Bastrop after they'd spent an entire night making love and committing to a future together tested her courage. Darn it, she wanted Drew to protest. To sweep her into his arms and confess that he'd made a mistake. That he wanted her by his side. But he'd already slipped into the role of the hard-as-nails cowboy.

"Hey, buddy. Got your gear together?" He ruffled Nick's hair, and she bit her lip at Drew's hurt expression when their son shrugged off his touch.

What had Drew expected when he was pushing them away? Then she reminded herself that he hadn't forced her to leave. She'd made the decision of her own free will.

"I don't want to go." Nick crossed his arms over his chest and pouted. She could see Nick's pathetic face wreaked havoc with his father. Drew rubbed his brow, then clenched and unclenched his fists.

"I'm sorry the trip got cut short, buddy. I'll see you real soon."

Nick scowled. "When are you gonna come home?"

Home. The word struck a sad chord inside Hallie.

"After the rodeo today." Drew squatted and hugged Nick's stiff body.

She wished Drew would reassure her that this impossible situation they were in would end well. But he wouldn't pull her close—there was too much yearning left over from their lovemaking to risk touching until they said their final goodbyes.

"Brody called. Your ride was moved up."

"To what time?"

"Noon."

"The rental car arrived while I was paying the bill." Drew glanced at his watch.

"You go ahead to the arena. Nick and I can manage the luggage."

"I wanted to follow you out of town and make sure you got on the interstate okay, but I won't have time for that."

"Nick, let's go, honey."

"I wanna watch cartoons."

Determined to keep her cool she reached for Nick's hand and tugged him off the bed. Nick resisted, digging his little boot heels into the carpet.

She tightened her grip and ignored the painful grimace on Drew's face when she and Nick marched from the room. Drew followed with the suitcases.

The elevator ride to the lobby was made in silence. She found no consolation in Drew's and Nick's misery and worried that the tension among the three of them would affect Drew's performance at the rodeo. The elevator doors whooshed open and Hallie touched Drew's shirtsleeve. "He'll be fine. He's stubborn like you."

Drew grinned. "That he is."

"You'll phone after your ride?" she asked, when they stopped next to the rental.

"Yep. I promise." He opened the trunk of the car and stowed the luggage, then helped Nick into the backseat and buckled him in. "Do you have enough money on you in case of an emergency?"

"Yes. Sharon's picking us up from the rental agency once we arrive in town." By the end of the day, she knew she'd need her friend's shoulder to cry on.

Drew kept staring at her mouth, and Hallie decided they were crazy for talking about mundane things when what they both wanted was a kiss. Good grief, this wasn't a forever goodbye. They'd see each other after Drew competed. Battling the sting of tears, she groped for the driver's-side door handle. She didn't want Drew's last image of her to be with puffy eyes and a blotchy face.

As if in slow motion his hand caressed her hair, tangling it around his fingers, coaxing her head toward his. He shielded her face with the brim of his Stetson. His mouth parted, moved closer, covered hers. Rough and a little forceful…desperate…wild. She needed to feel the same connection they'd experienced before dawn's light filtered through the motel window. His arms slid around her waist and he crushed her to him.

As suddenly as the kiss began, it ended, leaving her feeling as if she'd been sucked up and spit out of a passing dust devil. He poked his head into the backseat. "Be good for your mom, okay?"

Nick didn't answer. He was better at keeping a grudge than Hallie.

"I'm going to miss you, buddy." This time Nick didn't protest when his father hugged him.

Drew stepped back from the car. Like a fool Hallie waited, hoping he'd admit he loved her. A second, then two, then three passed. He tapped a finger against the brim of his hat. "Drive safe, Hallie."

Darn him. He rounded the front of the camper and stopped by the door. Their eyes met.

"Ride safe," she whispered.

He cranked the engine, then backed out of the parking spot and drove away without a honk or wave. After the camper turned onto the road and merged with traffic Hallie got into the rental car.

She glanced in the rearview mirror. Her son was as miserable as she was. Tears dribbled down Nick's cheeks. "Honey, I'm sad, too."

As she familiarized herself with the car's controls, anxiety began to build in her. The thought of driving down the interstate, wondering who'd come out on top—Gut Twister or Drew—was too much to bear. She couldn't leave the area until she knew for certain Drew was safe. She'd just have to make sure the cowboy never saw her and Nick in the stands before he competed. "How would you like to see your dad ride this afternoon?"

"Aw, right!" Nick's smile was worth any extra grief Drew would give her.

"READY?" BRODY ASKED.

"As I'll ever be." Drew paced the cowboy-ready area, his ears tuned to the snorts and whinnies of the rodeo stock.

"Thought you were gonna scratch. Didn't Hallie give you my message?" The bull rider dogged his heels.

The image of Hallie standing next to the rental car outside the motel was as bright as the arena lights burning down on him. "I got the message."

"What kept you?"

"Traffic," he lied. Drew inhaled the smells of rodeo— rank animals, manure, stale chew and dust. He willed the stink to chase Hallie from his mind, but her image was burned into his brain. It was a hell of a mess—him wanting her by his side, yet not being able to concentrate worth a damn when she was near.

"Do-or-die time, hoss." Brody slapped him on the shoulder.

A lot had happened in the past twenty minutes. Three of Drew's competitors had gotten bucked off and were out of the money race and even if Fitzgerald beat Drew's score there was a chance they could tie—as long as Drew lasted eight seconds in the saddle.

A victory today would ensure him a trip to the NFR and if he made it to Vegas, he wasn't leaving a loser. A man had few chances in life to ever reach his full potential, so before he retired his spurs and settled down with Hallie and Nick, he intended to give rodeo his all one more time.

If you get hurt today will you promise not to compete in Vegas?

Guilt slammed into Drew as Hallie's request reverberated inside his head. *If I can't ride, I'll quit.* Hadn't Hallie realized by now that nothing short of death would keep him from competing?

Drew stopped next to chute seven and secured his protective vest. He eyed Gut Twister. "The bronc looks nervous."

As if sensing the enemy, the gelding's glassy black eyes stared straight into Drew's soul. Drew broke out in a cold sweat.

"Got any idea how to stay on the bastard?" Brody asked.

"Park my ass in the saddle and hold the buck-rein until the beast yanks my arm out of the socket."

"That'll work." Concern darkened Brody's eyes.

"Quit worrying. Me and Gut Twister are gonna get along fine." Drew reached through the slats and slapped the bronc's rump. He heard his name announced. The arena clamor faded to background noise as he climbed the chute. Taking a cautious breath, he settled in the saddle. The gelding froze—not even a quiver ran through its body. *Bad sign.*

Closing his eyes, Drew waited for his first surge of adrenaline to hit him, but felt only a trickle of nervous tension. The tangy scent of sweat clung to his clothes, and he was certain the horse smelled his fear.

"All eyes on chute seven. Drew Rawlins from San Antonio is comin' out on Gut Twister!" The fans exploded with applause and loud music thundered through the center. After a minute the music faded and the crowd quieted. Drew focused his thoughts inward, only hearing bits and pieces of the announcer's commentary—a recap of his rib injury, his age, his fall in the standings and this ride being his last chance to make it to the finals.

He heard just enough to shake his confidence.

Since Drew had become involved with Hallie his focus on rodeo had grown hazy around the edges, as if he were just going through the motions.

Gripping the rein tighter, he concentrated on the feel of the rope around his glove and the fifteen hundred pounds of TNT wedged between his thighs.

After a moment, only the gelding's labored breathing filtered into Drew's ears. The anticipation of conquering the unconquerable finally triggered a release of adrenaline. Drew closed his eyes and pictured the ride in his mind.... His left hand gripping the rein, his right hand high in the air above his head. His legs spurring the horse out of the chute. His body loose and limber, flowing, bending with each buck and twist. A specter with long blond hair and somber brown eyes materialized in his vision, rocking him back in the saddle. Drew shook his head to rid his mind of Hallie's face at the same time the gate opened and Gut Twister bolted from the chute.

Unprepared for the jolt, Drew almost lost his seat. Sheer instinct and years of riding made him raise his spurs high against the bronc's shoulder's and hold them there until the front hooves hit the ground outside the chute. His thigh muscles burned as he fought to keep his balance.

The horse swung right, all four hooves slashing the air. Drew clenched his jaw until his teeth threatened to shatter. When the beast crashed to the ground, the impact cut through his ribs like a handsaw.

The harried rhythm of the bronc's labored breathing echoed Drew's desperate need for air. The gelding flailed his forelegs. Clinging to ninety percent bull-headedness and ten percent sheer luck, Drew managed to keep his seat.

Gut Twister back-jumped, slamming his rear hooves against the dirt. Drew clutched the rope tighter and ignored the pain engulfing his body like a firestorm. Sweat poured down his face, burning his eyes. He fought to keep them open, needing to gauge the enemy's next move. Drew lost track of time and place, aware of only physical sensation—pain. The buzzer sounded, and the pickup men rode toward him. He held on through another round of brutal twisting.

Quickly he worked the rope free of his glove and leaned to the right where help waited. But the moment he reached out, Gut Twister lifted his hind legs and sent a swift, calculated kick at the other horse.

The friendly hand disappeared, and suddenly nothing stood between Drew and the ground but thin air. He landed on his shoulder and hip, his breath exploding from his chest. Automatically, he raised his arms to shield his head, the simple motion excruciatingly painful.

Choking on dust, he didn't know which way to roll. The horses had him boxed in and hooves slashed the air above his head.

Damn. He curled into a ball.

He expected it—was almost relieved when it finally happened. A hoof struck him in the side. Numbness worked through his body, filling his limbs until the only sensation that remained was the pounding of his heart.

"Hell of a ride, man. Ain't never seen nothing like it."

The pickup man lifted Drew's arms from around his head. "Hold on, cowboy. We got help comin'."

Drew's vision closed off, as shadows moved around him. *What's my score, damn it!* He couldn't get the words past his lips.

"Drew? Can you hear me?"

He recognized Brody's voice and nodded.

"You did it, man. You went out a winner on Gut Twister."

Thank God. He wasn't washed up yet.

A paramedic slipped a brace around his neck and a body board beneath him. He concentrated on taking shallow breaths as they carried him to the ambulance. He'd probably fractured more ribs—the least of his worries. Hallie was going to be pissed as hell when he told her about this. Then again, maybe she was better off not knowing.

Chapter Thirteen

Hallie's stomach churned with nausea.

Large air vents in the ceiling circulated the smell of disinfectant through the E.R. waiting room. After working as a nurse for six years she should have been immune to the sickly sweet odor.

A half hour had passed since she'd arrived at the hospital and no word yet on Drew's condition. Thankfully, a hospital volunteer had taken Nick to the cafeteria for a snack and Hallie no longer had to field questions about Drew—questions she didn't have answers for.

Is Dad gonna be okay?

Is Dad hurt bad?

How come we can't see Dad?

At the sound of heavy footfalls in the corridor Hallie sprang from her chair. Brody stepped into the room. Disappointment, sharp and biting, sucked the air from her lungs.

"Any news?" Brody removed his hat.

"Not yet." She wanted to say no news is good news but she'd worked enough shifts in the E.R. to understand that scenario wasn't always true.

"Drew said you and Nick had left for Bastrop before

the rodeo." Brody crossed the room and stopped in front of the windows overlooking the parking lot.

"I changed my mind and decided to take Nick to see his father ride before heading home." Thank goodness she'd gone to the American Airlines Center. Who knew how long she'd have waited to hear from Drew or anyone else regarding his injuries.

"Where's Nick?"

"In the cafeteria with a hospital volunteer. How did your ride go?"

He blinked as if her question took him by surprise. "Same as always—couldn't keep my seat." A stilted silence followed, Brody avoiding eye contact.

"Drew's quitting rodeo." There. She'd said it. Out loud.

The bull rider's mouth sagged open, then he snapped it shut. "Drew can't quit. The finals are next month."

"He promised to retire if he suffered a serious injury." Drew had better keep his promise. "Today's fall qualifies as serious."

"You're overreacting." Brody paced.

She cut him off at the pass. "Drew's been riding with injuries since the Bastrop rodeo. His body can't take any more abuse."

"Drew knows his physical limits."

"If he competes in Vegas and ends up dead, will you accuse me of overreacting?"

The blood drained from Brody's face, leaving his skin pale. Shame brought tears to her eyes. She'd been strong until now. Brody's hands clamped onto her shoulders and pulled her close. Her nose bumped into a wall of sinew and muscle. Darn it. She didn't want this man's sympathy.

The gravelly sound of a throat clearing echoed through the room and Hallie stepped away from Brody. A short, gaunt man with thinning gray hair and wire-rimmed glasses weaved through the seating area. He carried an X-ray in one hand and a medical chart in the other. "Are you relatives of—" he glanced at the chart "—Drew Rawlins?"

"I'm his fiancée." Hallie ignored Brody's raised eyebrow.

"Dr. Morgan." He offered his hand.

Hallie motioned to Brody. "This is Brody Murphy, Drew's close friend."

"Mr. Rawlins has been admitted," the doctor said.

A mix of fear and relief filled Hallie. Fear that Drew's injuries were far more severe than she'd assumed and relief that as long as he remained in the hospital, busting broncs was out of the question.

"Your fiancé has a history of fractures." The doctor waved the X-ray. "There's evidence of bone calcifications on several ribs. But my greatest concern at the moment is the uneven chest movement on his right side when he breathes."

Uneven chest movements meant that Drew's ribs were fractured in more than one place, making the bones unable to support the chest wall.

"Mr. Rawlins said he cracked a rib back in—" the doctor flipped the chart open "—August."

"Yes, he did."

"That same rib is broken in two places."

Hallie glanced at Brody, but the bull rider had turned his back on the doctor and stared out the windows.

"There's a slight rattle in his lungs," the doctor continued.

Pneumonia. Why didn't Drew tell her he was having trouble breathing?

"I've put him on antibiotics, but I'd like him to remain in the hospital until his lungs clear." The doctor glanced between Hallie and Brody. "Do you have any questions?"

"You told Drew he couldn't rodeo anymore, right, Doctor?" Hallie asked.

"I advised against any physical activity for a minimum of six weeks."

Drew wouldn't be in any shape to compete in Vegas. Hallie hated to see him suffer painful injuries, but she'd be a liar if she didn't admit that she was relieved his quest for the title had come to an end. Finally, she and Drew could make plans for the future.

"Mr. Rawlins is in room 324. He needs his rest so keep your visits short."

After the doctor left, Brody spoke. "Hallie, I need to get on the road. Would you mind if I saw Drew first? I'll make it quick."

"Go ahead." Now that Hallie knew Drew would be okay, she needed time to gather her composure. Alone in the waiting room, she sank into a chair and struggled against the fear gripping her belly. Today she could have lost Drew—the father of her son. The man she'd fallen hopelessly in love with. She took solace in the knowledge that from this moment on rodeo no longer stood in her way of a happily-ever-after with Drew. Today, she, Nick and Drew could start being a real family.

"YOU AWAKE, HOSS?"

Drew forced his eyelids open. The blurry form at the end of his bed slowly came into focus. *Brody.* "Tell me you didn't call Hallie."

"Didn't have to. She was there. She saw everything."

Drew groaned—not from pain. "Where is she?"

"Waiting room."

"You win?" Drew forced a smile.

Brody scoffed. "What do you think?"

"The doctor didn't lie, did he? I'm gonna be okay, right?"

"As long as you give yourself time to heal." Brody's face was pale, his eyes hollow. "I gotta have my say, Drew. I've tried to stay out of your business but—" he shook his head "—you're the closest thing to a brother I've got and I don't want to see you get hurt."

"I'm listening."

"Hallie told the doctor she was your fiancée."

"I didn't have a chance to tell you, but Hallie agreed to marry me."

"Why do you want to get married?"

Drew frowned. "Because I love Hallie and Nick and want us to be a family. I'm tired of being a father who shows up every couple of weeks to take his son to supper or watch a movie with him."

"Don't go down that road, Drew. It leads straight to hell."

"You think it's a mistake for me to commit to Hallie and Nick?"

"I lost a daughter." Brody stared at the tips of his boots. "A little girl who depended on me to keep her safe. I had a wife who expected me to make the right decisions for our family. I had everything a man could want, but it wasn't enough. I wanted more. I wanted to do what was in my best interest. I put me first. That would have been okay if I hadn't had a family."

Brody remained silent for a long while, before he spoke in a hoarse voice. "Because I did what I wanted, I lost both a wife and a daughter." Brody glanced up, his eyes glistening with emotion. "You're one of the best at bustin' broncs, Drew. Take my advice—stick to what you do best. Keep on rodeoing and forget about settling down with Hallie and Nick. It'll save you and them a lot of pain in the long run."

Drew didn't have a chance to process Brody's words before the door opened and Hallie walked in.

"Get well, hoss." Brody left the room without another word.

Hallie watched Brody's retreating back as he hurried toward the elevators. The bleak expression on his face had sent chills down her spine. What in the world had the two men discussed?

She moved closer to Drew's bed, where he lay beneath a thin blue blanket. The curtains had been drawn against the afternoon sun, and the fluorescent light above the bed cast a sickly yellow hue over his face.

An IV pumped medicine into the back of Drew's right hand. A large gauze bandage covered his elbow— he must have scraped it against the ground when he'd fallen. The vulnerable, weak man lying in the bed was a far cry from the larger-than-life cowboy she'd come to love.

And that frightened her.

"Where's Nick?" he asked.

"Playing cards with a volunteer in the waiting room."

"You stayed."

Hallie nodded. "Nick wanted to watch you ride and I needed to make sure you were okay before I left town." She thought Drew might be ticked off at her, but he let the subject drop.

"Did the doc say how soon I can ride again?"

Drew's main concern was rodeo—not what she and Nick had suffered through after witnessing his close call today? She clasped Drew's hand, needing to feel connected to him. "The doctor said no physical activity for a minimum of six weeks."

He squeezed her hand. "I don't feel that bad."

"Because you're on pain meds." Gently she rubbed his scraped knuckles.

"I'm gonna be okay," he insisted.

"Yes, you are. I'll make sure of it this time."

"Did the doc say anything else?"

"You've got a touch of pneumonia and he wants you to remain in the hospital until he's sure the antibiotics are working."

"I won today." Drew's eyes begged for understanding.

"I know, but you also broke your ribs."

Drew released her hand, curling his fingers into a

fist. "The ribs will heal well enough to compete in a few weeks. They'll hold up for one more go-round."

One more? If he survived the first go-round in Vegas he'd need nine more rides to win the title. "Your ribs can't survive that kind of abuse."

"I know what my body can take and what it can't." He pressed his palm to his side. "This doesn't *feel* like serious to me."

The desperate note in his voice scared Hallie. "Drew, for once follow the doctor's advice."

He shook his head. "Three weeks of solid rest. No riding. I'll be good as new."

Anger and frustration bubbled to the surface as she studied his haggard face, noting the dark smudges beneath his eyes and the scratches on his cheek. "Wouldn't it be easier and a lot less painful to put a gun to your head?"

Drew sucked in a harsh breath.

"I'm sorry. I shouldn't have said that. But I'm worried about you." The urge to bawl was strong, but she shoved the emotion aside.

His fingers tangled in her hair, and he pulled her close, until her lips hovered over his mouth. "You shouldn't have stayed."

"Nick was so scared, Drew."

"It isn't every day a kid sees his father lying in the dirt while a horse dances on top of him." Drew's mouth inched closer. "I'm sorry I frightened you." Under any other circumstance his kiss would have eased her fears, but right now the caress made her anxious.

He nuzzled her cheek, then whispered, "I'm gonna win the big one. You'll see."

She pulled free of his grasp and retreated to the foot of the bed.

"I've still got a shot at the title."

The title. Her chest tightened with a horrible, sickening sensation. "What about our future?"

"Winning the title comes with a big purse. Money I can use to invest in Dry Creek Acres and get my horse-breeding operation off the ground." He cleared his throat. "I want to be a good provider for you and Nick. And I want my son to be proud of me. I want him to understand his father isn't a quitter."

The blood pumping through Hallie's veins slowed to a trickle. Didn't he know she loved *him*—not what he could give her? "I don't need a man to take care of me, Drew. I need a man to love me."

"C'mere." He held out his hand. She inched her way up to his pillow. "A man needs to know he can provide for his family."

Drew might be stubborn and complicated, but Hallie loved him nonetheless. She'd walked away from him five years ago and wasn't about to desert him again—she had to save Drew from himself. "I've got a 401K we can use to invest in the ranch." Invest in their future.

"I won't take your money."

What kind of a relationship did they have if he didn't see her as an equal? A deep sadness filled Hallie at the realization that Drew would never love her as much as he loved rodeo. Even so, she had to find a way to stop him from competing—Nick would be crushed if he lost his father after just being reunited with him.

"Please, Drew. Let me help," she begged.

"I'm doing this my way."

"It's all about you, isn't it?"

"Hallie—"

"I told myself it would be a mistake falling for a cowboy—"

"Mind if we save the arguing for later?"

"We're not arguing. We're talking about our future, which happens to be very important to me."

"The future will take care of itself. Don't worry."

She crossed her arms over her chest to conceal her thundering heart. "If I ask you a question, will you tell me the truth?" At his nod she asked, "What's really driving you to take chances with your life?"

He smoothed a hand over the blanket. "I have a score to settle with my father."

"You're doing this because of a dead man."

Fire sparked in his eyes. "I'm gonna prove to my old man that I've got what it takes to be a world champion."

What about her and Nick? Didn't they count for anything? She should leave. Walk away…this time for good. But how could she let Drew go when everything inside her insisted he was her future. She swallowed the nauseating fear rising in her throat.

"Hallie? Are you all right?"

"No." She stared at his face, yearning to caress his cheek and savor the scratchy feel of his five o'clock shadow. "Do you have any idea how helpless it feels to watch the man you love almost die? For a split second to not know if that person is dead or alive?"

"A few more weeks and I'll retire for real."

"What about your promise?"

The brightness in his blue eyes dimmed. "What promise?"

"The one you made in the motel room. You said you'd quit if you suffered a serious injury." Drew remained silent. "You're going back on your word, aren't you?"

"I'm not a cripple."

"In other words, when you made that promise you were counting on being dead in order to keep it."

"Something like that," he muttered.

He'd shattered her trust. "How do you expect me to believe you'll really quit after the finals if you're going back on your promise now?"

"I've spent my whole life working toward this opportunity. Most cowboys only dream of going to Vegas. I'm there, Hallie. I have to see this journey through."

"Even if your dream costs you your life? Costs a little boy his father?" *Costs me the man I love?*

"You're being melodramatic."

Second best. That's all she'd ever be to Drew. Well, she wasn't willing to settle for second best. And Nick deserved better, too. "This isn't going to work."

"What are you talking about?"

"You. Me."

"You, me, what? Spell it out, Hallie."

Time to end the visit. Drew needed his rest and she needed a good cry. "We're finished, Drew."

"Finished, how?"

Heart breaking, she brushed a dark strand of hair from his forehead. "We can be friends, but I'm not risking my heart on you."

"Friends don't sleep with one another. And friends don't kiss like this." He snaked his hand through her hair and pulled her face close. His tongue snuck into her mouth, teasing and taunting. "One more rodeo. That's all I'm asking for."

Heart aching, Hallie headed for the door. "I'm sorry, Drew. I can't stand by you any longer."

"You're being selfish. Three weeks and a little patience isn't much to ask for."

"Wanting a home and a healthy family is far from selfish."

"What about what I want?" He poked his chest with his finger. "Okay, yeah, I want the title for selfish reasons—me. But you and Nick showed up late in the game—that's not my fault. That's your fault, Hallie. You were the one who kept my son a secret from me."

Drew was right. If he hadn't run into her and Nick at the hospital back in August this conversation wouldn't even be taking place. Still, she held out hope that Drew would forgive her for her past mistakes. "It's Nick and me, or rodeo."

The silence that reverberated throughout the room was answer enough. She reached for the door handle.

"Stop right there, Hallie. You're not running away from me again."

If she wasn't so close to tears she might laugh at his male arrogance.

"You want my soul, don't you?" His voice broke.

Hallie glanced over her shoulder. "I deserve as much."

"What if I can't give you my soul?"

She remembered the day she'd stood in front of the judge, listening to her father give a hundred excuses why he didn't want custody of her. She'd never believed she'd ever feel that kind of agony again. She'd been wrong. The pain she felt the day her father had abandoned her paled in comparison to the hurt ripping her apart now.

"What about Nick?" His eyes darkened with anxiety.

She ached for the family she'd hoped they'd become. "You'll always be his father. You can visit him as much as you want."

"Are you driving back to Bastrop?"

She wondered what he feared most—letting her go or begging her to stay? "Yes. Nick and I are going home."

"You don't understand. Asking me to quit now is like telling a man who's a hundred yards from the top of Mount Everest that he has to turn around and climb down the mountain." He pinched the bridge of his nose and closed his eyes. When he opened them, Hallie saw straight to the bottom of his soul.

"Tell me to quit right now and I will." The catch in Drew's voice brought tears to her eyes.

Drew might be okay with quitting today and tomorrow. But a year from now he'd blame her for making him give up on his dream. Funny how her love for Drew was the key to his freedom.

"I won't tell you to quit." *Because I love you enough to let you go.*

"So, this is the end?"

She waited before responding—for what, she wasn't sure. A sign. A word. A look.

Nothing. "Keep in touch," she said.

"Yeah. I'll send a postcard."

She stiffened at the cutting remark.

"I never pegged you for a quitter, Hallie."

She left the room, Drew's words piercing her heart and echoing in her ears all the way back to the waiting room.

Chapter Fourteen

Vegas.

Three long, miserable weeks missing Hallie and Nick was nearing an end. In two days his life would move in a different direction—one he hoped would lead him back to Hallie. He was tired of lying alone at night dreaming of her smile, her touch. Her kiss.

God, he missed her.

And he missed his son.

Thanksgiving had come and gone without Hallie and Nick. He'd reinvited them to share the holiday with him at his mother's home, where he'd recuperated after the rodeo in Dallas. Hallie had turned down the invitation. Not even a call from his mother had changed her mind. He guessed he should be grateful Hallie allowed him to speak with Nick when he phoned.

The calls had become more stressful than ever. He loved hearing his son's voice, and he didn't have to be present to see his absence was taking a toll on Nick. Nick's feelings were hurt that Drew hadn't stopped by the apartment since the road trip. Each time he spoke with Nick, the boy's voice became more and more subdued as if he believed his father no longer cared about him. The whole situation was tearing Drew apart.

What had he expected? He'd gone back on his promise.

A cold sweat broke across his brow at the possibility that Hallie really meant to end their relationship. He wished she'd been in Vegas this past week to watch him ride at the Thomas and Mack Center on the University of Nevada campus. He'd stunned the competition and had won seven out of the eight go-rounds, moving him into second place behind Fitzgerald.

Two more winning rides and he'd walk away a world champion. Most cowboys would be sweating bullets under the pressure—not Drew. As long as he remained focused and kept his butt in the saddle, the title was within reach.

"Hey, Drew!" Brody weaved his way through a throng of milling rodeo fans, wannabe cowboys and competitors. "What do you say we hit the strip with the guys and celebrate?"

"I don't think so, hoss." No one—not even Brody—was aware of how badly Drew's ribs ached. After his injury in Dallas, he'd taken the doctor's advice to heart and had spent the weeks leading up to the NFR flat on his back in his mother's guest bedroom. Drew decided the only reason he managed to walk upright this week was because he hadn't been tossed on his backside.

"C'mon, Drew. You're a celebrity now."

Drew was well aware he'd surprised his competition

and the media with his streak of good luck this week. He wondered what the reporters would write about him if they discovered he was riding with cracked ribs. "Not tonight, Brody." He wanted to phone Hallie and Nick. He needed to hear their voices. To feel connected to them.

"Hey, Rawlins!" Riley Fitzgerald approached. "See you brought your cheering section with you to Vegas." He winked at Brody.

"I'm outta here." Brody stomped off.

Willing his stomach to settle, Drew tightened his grip on his gear bag. He wasn't sure if it was the smell of burnt popcorn or Fitzgerald's cockiness that caused the sudden onset of queasiness.

"That arthritis medicine you're taking for old age must have some zip in it," Fitzgerald said. "Why your ass looked downright tickled in the saddle today." The black-haired nuisance was pissed.

"Ought to try some." Drew grinned. "Beats the hell out of those Flintstone vitamins you take." The cowpokes near the turnstiles overheard the banter and guffawed. Fitzgerald's face reddened.

"You're riding on nothing but luck, Rawlins. Pure luck." The young hothead inched closer until the brim of his hat bumped Drew's. "Tomorrow, your luck runs out."

"We'll see about that." Drew headed toward the exit.

"You'll see, old man. I'm stealing the title right out from under your spurs."

Drew kept walking.

"I don't like you, Rawlins. Even if you do have a crapload of courage."

Drew's long strides slowed. If only the braggart realized it took more courage to walk away and quit rodeo than it did to ride a bronc with injured ribs day after day.

It had taken the sum total of three weeks—twenty-one days of gut-level loneliness—to force Drew to look deep inside himself. At night, lying in the dark, he struggled to understand why he cared so much about proving his father wrong. Winning a world title had always been his father's dream. Half the time Drew didn't even know who he was riding for anymore, himself or his father. Was it he or his father who believed his worth was defined by whether or not he won a national title?

The most frightening thought that banged around inside Drew's head was the very real possibility that it was too late to win Hallie and Nick back. Hallie had insisted Drew would be welcome in Nick's life, but what if she changed her mind and she didn't want Drew anywhere near their son?

No, damn it. She gave me her word.

Drew blanched. How the hell did he expect Hallie to keep her word when he'd gone back on his? He stepped outside the arena and moved away from the door. Leaning against the wall, he phoned Hallie's apartment. After three rings he checked his watch. Where was she at seven-thirty on a Thursday night?

Five rings.

C'mon, Hallie. Answer the phone.

Seven rings.

He closed his eyes, knowing the answering machine would kick in on the eighth ring.

"Hello?"

Startled by the sound of her voice, Drew almost dropped his phone. "Hey. It's me."

"Drew?"

Who else would allow the phone to ring that long? "You and Nick okay?"

"Nick's fine."

What about you, Hallie? "What are you guys up to?" Maybe if he acted as if Dallas had never happened she would, too.

"We went to an early showing of a Disney movie after Nick got out of school today." Hallie didn't elaborate.

"ESPN can't compete with Disney."

A soft sigh echoed in his ear. "What do you want, Drew?"

Although deserved, he hated the suspicious note in her voice. He didn't blame her for wanting to make him pay for breaking his promise. He understood her fear that he'd abandon her and Nick the way her father had. Maybe not exactly the same way—dying was different than walking out on a person.

"I'm in second place behind Fitzgerald. If I win tomorrow, we'll be tied going into the finals on Saturday."

"I know. I searched the NFR website and found a link to live updates."

She cares.

"How are your ribs?"

"Fine. Helps when you don't get bucked off." His

attempt at humor fell flat. He wanted to keep her talking, so he could pretend she was next to him instead of a thousand miles away. Then during the darkest hours of the night when his loneliness woke him he'd replay their conversation in his mind until the memory of her voice lulled him back to sleep. "How's Nick doing in preschool?"

"His Christmas program is next Thursday."

Was it only this past August that he'd met his son for the first time? The anger, the hurt, the resentment he'd harbored toward Hallie for keeping Nick a secret had withered away with time. The courage it had taken Hallie to offer him a place in their lives humbled Drew, but he wanted more. He wanted the three of them to be a real family. He wanted Hallie's heart.

Hallie had made sacrifices so Drew could be with Nick, but what had he given up to help the puzzle pieces of their lives fit better? *Nothing.*

Not one damned thing.

"I need to go." Hallie's words interrupted Drew's musings.

"Can I talk to Nick?"

"He's getting ready for bed."

"I'll make it quick."

"Fine."

While Drew waited for Nick to come to the phone, he wondered what the heck he had to do to show Hallie that he loved her and that they belonged together. Then it blindsided him. Hallie didn't know how much he needed her in his life. He'd never wined and dined her. They'd never been on a date by themselves. He'd never spoken soft words in her ear when they *weren't* making love. He'd never told her how much he needed her in his life. How could he expect her to know he couldn't live without her when he hadn't told her?

At the moment, rodeo came first in his life, but Hallie would always be first in his heart.

He gambled his life on his instincts. Instinct kept him alive in the arena more times than he cared to remember. That same intuition told him Hallie hadn't walked out on him in Dallas because she didn't love him—she'd walked out on him because she'd believed he loved rodeo more than her.

His hand patted the object in the front pocket of his Wranglers. He'd bought the ring in a pawnshop on the Vegas strip when he'd first arrived in town. The antique silver wedding band had sparkled in the window as he'd strolled by. At first he'd admired the ornate ring. Then he'd wondered how it would look on Hallie's finger. Like him, the ring had been waiting for a second chance. After the finals, he'd show Hallie he was committed to their future. For once in his life he'd put others before himself.

If it wasn't already too late.

"Hi, Dad."

Drew winced at the lack of enthusiasm in his son's voice. "How are you, buddy?"

No answer.

"How was the movie?"

"Mom cried."

"Cried at a Disney movie?"

"She cries a lot."

The whispered words hugged Drew's bruised and battered heart. "Why does she cry?"

"'Cause she said we have the same faces."

Hallie missed him. God, he prayed it was so, because he couldn't live without her. "We do look alike, buddy."

"Are you comin' to my Christmas party? We're gonna sing songs and I made you a Christmas present."

Drew swallowed the lump in his throat. This was the most Nick had said to him since Dallas. If things didn't work out between him and Hallie he hoped to God he'd still have Nick.

"I'll be at your party, son."

"Mom says I gotta hang up 'n' take a bath. Don't forget my party."

"I won't." Drew gripped the phone tighter, wanting to stay connected to Nick a little longer....

"'Bye."

"Love you, Nick."

Disappointment, sharp and biting, filled him when the dial tone buzzed in his ear. He pushed number three on his speed dial.

This time Hallie answered after one ring.

"Damn it, Hallie. You gotta know I love you more than rodeo." He snapped his cell phone closed, not willing to find out if she'd say the words back to him.

Coward.

He loves me.

Drew's confession knocked the wind from Hallie's lungs. She'd convinced herself these past few weeks that if Drew really cared for her he would have kept his promise and retired after getting hurt in Dallas. But there had been no mistaking the raw emotion in his voice when he'd called back and confessed he loved her.

Darn it.

Hallie wished she hadn't answered the phone. A few simple words from Drew and the wall she'd erected around her heart had crumbled. When she'd left Drew's hospital room, Hallie had never expected to be this lonely, this lost, without him.

At night while she lay alone in bed her memory replayed every thought, word, gesture and look that had passed between her and Drew in Dallas. Each night she'd come to the same conclusion—she'd left him out of fear.

Fear for him.

Fear of living her life without him.

Fear of committing to a man she might have to bury before his time.

Hallie heard the sound of water filling the tub in the bathroom and resisted the urge to check on Nick. He'd informed her a short while ago that Jason took baths by himself and didn't need his mom's help. She suspected Nick's sudden streak of independence had less to do with his school friend and more to do with a desire for longer playtime in the water.

She crossed the living room, beckoned by the photograph Sharon had taken of her, Drew and Nick next to the camper before the start of their road trip.

Nick stood between her and Drew, gazing up at his

father with hero worship in his eyes. Hallie's smile had been forced—she'd been filled with reservations about the trip but determined not to back out.

Drew's piercing blue eyes rested on her with a fierce possessiveness that even now made her knees weak. He might not love her in the all-consuming, self-sacrificing way she yearned to be loved, but he loved her as much as he was capable of.

More importantly, Drew loved Nick. Her son had a father who wanted to be with him. Had she forgotten how she'd longed for a father's love all her life? When had she turned so selfish? When had her needs suddenly been more important than the needs of the two people she loved most? Shame brought tears to her eyes.

She wiped away the moisture on her cheek then checked on Nick. Mounds of bubbles filled the tub. "I'm not done."

"Did you wash behind your ears?"

"No."

"Hand me the sponge." She knelt on the bath mat and scrubbed his neck and back.

"Dad said he's gonna come to my Christmas party." After weeks of the dreary doldrums, tantrums and pure orneriness, the hint of excitement in Nick's voice was a pleasant change.

"He'll be there, honey." Nothing short of a disaster would prevent Drew from making it to Nick's school.

It was time Hallie accepted the truth. She wasn't enough for her son. Nick needed both a mother and a father—each loving and nurturing him in their own special way.

She trusted Drew wholeheartedly with Nick's well-being, but when it came to her heart, she balked. She hated that her father's neglect made her afraid to trust.

Drew won't walk away from you.

Then there were the flowers. Drew had sent a dozen roses two days after she'd left his hospital room in Dallas.

Don't forget his phone calls. Drew might not have visited her and Nick in three weeks, but not a day went by that he didn't phone them.

She forced herself to view the situation from Drew's perspective. He was good at riding broncs. Darn good. What would she do if she was told she couldn't be a nurse any longer? Couldn't help the injured or sick?

I'd tell them to take a flying leap.

Rodeo and Drew were so tightly entwined she didn't know where one stopped and the other began. The sport had been a major influence on his life and made him the man he was today—courageous, prideful, determined. She'd give anything to change the way he felt about rodeo, but she sympathized with his desire to finish the journey he'd begun years ago long before he met her. Still, he'd broken her heart when he'd gone back on his promise to retire if he suffered a serious injury.

You committed a worse sin.

Hallie had done the unthinkable when she didn't contact Drew after she became pregnant. She'd purposefully excluded him from her and Nick's lives until fate had revealed her secret.

Drew wasn't trying to exclude her from his life. He was trying to include her in every way possible.

She'd always assumed if she believed in her heart's desire long enough she'd get it. And she definitely believed the three of them were meant to be a family. The time had come to take a leap of faith. To jump in with both feet as Sharon had once suggested.

But this time when she jumped, she had to trust Drew would catch her.

Tears of relief and happiness sprang to her eyes.

"Aw, Mom. Are you gonna cry again?"

Laughter bubbled inside her chest. "How would you like to watch your father ride in Las Vegas on Saturday?"

"Yesss!" Nick slapped the water with his hand, and soap bubbles spewed into the air.

Now that Hallie had come to her senses, she prayed fate wouldn't steal their chance to become a real family.

"SOUTHERN NIGHTS doesn't look particularly happy." Brody motioned to the horse being led into chute three.

"We're going to get along fine. Wait and see." Drew eyed the animal—part draft horse, part paint—and shook off the twinge of unease inching up his spine. Southern Nights had thrown every cowboy at the NFR, including Fitzgerald. Drew would be relieved when he and the bucking horse ended their association for good.

This morning on the way to the coliseum Drew had decided that no matter what happened in the arena today, he was through.

Finished.

Done with rodeo.

A mere eight seconds stood between him and a world title. He closed his eyes and willed his adrenaline to kick in—nothing but a trickle leaked into his veins. What the hell was the matter with him? Fitzgerald scored a seventy-nine on his ride. All Drew needed was an eighty to win. Shoot, he could ride blindfolded and score an eighty—as long as he didn't get bucked off.

Drew inched closer to the caged horse and stared into glassy black eyes—eyes that glowed with madness around the edges.

Brody nodded to the animal. "He swings to the right after coming out of the chute."

"I know." Southern Nights was predictable if nothing else.

"Likes to buck with his back legs."

"I know."

"He's not afraid to spin and—"

"I can handle him, Brody." Deep in his bones, Drew believed he'd outsmart Southern Nights as long as he didn't fight the animal.

In a matter of minutes, he'd earn the title of world champion, then he'd hightail it to Bastrop. He wouldn't give up until he'd made a place for himself in Hallie's and Nick's lives. "You have Hallie's number, right?" Drew drilled Brody with a steady stare.

"Jeez, hoss, you act like you're marching off to war."

Deep in his bones, Drew believed the ride would go off without a hitch, but there was always a chance... Last night he'd written two letters—short and sweet. He'd wanted the most important people in his life to know how much he loved them.

"I got the letters right here." Brody patted his shirt pocket. "I'm watching this show from the stands." He clasped Drew's hand, then walked off.

While Drew waited for the announcer to go through all the pomp and circumstance, his thoughts drifted to Hallie. God, he wished she were here. Nick, too. He wanted his son to see him walk across the arena and lift the trophy high above his head. He wanted those he loved to witness the one moment he was willing to risk his life for.

Stunned by that fleeting thought, Drew froze in the process of putting on his riding glove. What the hell kind of a man was he? His father had taught him that the measure of a man was what he had to show for years of hard work. Now, Drew wondered if a man's worth ought to be measured by the journey, not the end result.

He rubbed his forehead. The minor ache he'd woken up with exploded into a full-blown throb. In his quest for a world title he'd sacrificed a lot. And he'd driven away those who meant the most to him.

At that moment—with thousands of fans listening to the commentator proclaim him a bronc-busting super-hero—Drew hated himself.

He was no hero. He was a selfish son of a bitch. A real hero put the needs and wants of those he loved first. If Hallie didn't take him back after today, he'd be nothing but a lonely winner with a broken heart.

Out of sheer habit, he swung a leg over the chute rail. When his butt hit the saddle, he expected Southern Nights to tense up. The horse stood steady as if he knew the outcome before Drew did.

Drew pulled his hat low, twisted the buck rein around his hand and pounded the top of his fist, until the rope was one with his hand. He shrank inside himself, retreating to a place in his mind where only he and Southern Nights fit—but an image of Hallie stood between him and the gelding.

Frustrated, he opened his eyes and glanced around, waiting for the familiar adrenaline rush. He felt nothing but a deep sense of longing. For Hallie.

Shock freeze-dried the air in his lungs. He didn't want the trophy. He didn't want the money. He didn't want the prestigious title. He didn't even care anymore about proving his father wrong.

Faster than he'd moved in years, Drew hopped off Southern Nights and climbed down the rails. The announcer stopped in midsentence. The mouths of the cowboys around him dropped open.

When his boots hit the dirt outside the chute, a sense of rightness filled Drew. He hefted his gear bag onto his shoulder, then froze in place before he'd taken his first step.

Hallie?

Standing thirty feet away she held Nick's hand.

God damn. His throat clogged and his chest pounded until he thought his heart would explode. He fought to keep his eyes from watering in front of the whole frickin' world.

"Dad!"

Nick broke away from Hallie's hold and ran toward him. Relief, anxiety, fear, happiness warred inside him. He knelt down and felt the impact of Nick's little body slam into his. He hugged his son close.

Hallie hung back, causing a sliver of fear to work its way beneath Drew's skin. Had she come to Vegas to say a final goodbye? Drew tucked Nick against his side and forced his legs to move forward.

Hallie's brown eyes shimmered. "I should have come sooner."

He cleared his throat. "I'd say you're just in time."

Drew ignored the unnatural pall hanging over the coliseum. Every cowboy within a hundred feet stared as if he and Hallie were a mirage.

A loud buzzer echoed through the arena and Hallie jumped.

The announcer's voice cut through the thick silence. "Well, folks, in all my years announcing I've never seen anything like this before. It looks as if Drew Rawlins has scratched. This year's world bronc-bustin' title goes to Riley Fitzgerald by default."

The crowd's applause was reluctant at best.

Hallie nibbled her lower lip. "Why?"

"I'm nothing more than a broken-down cowboy, Hallie. But I'm standing here in front of the whole world begging you to give me a second chance."

She clutched his arm. "The title."

He rubbed a finger across her quivering lip. "I've never let anything but rodeo have this much power over me." He moved his finger to her cheek and caught a tear. "Until you walked out on me in Dallas, I never admitted to myself how much I'd given up. How much I'd sacrificed. You mean more to me than a damned title." He feathered a kiss across her mouth. "I don't want to be a world-champion cowboy. I want to be a world-champion husband and father. I love you, Hallie. Please marry me."

Tears rolled down her face. "Yes, I'll marry you. I love you, Drew." She caressed his cheek. "But that ride was your destiny."

He shook his head. "You're my destiny." He hugged her, then grasped Nick's hand. "C'mon, sport. Let's go home."

This time for good.

* * * * *

Look for Marin Thomas's next Rodeo Rebels story—
A BULL RIDER'S SECRET,
featuring Brody Murphy!
Available wherever Harlequin's books are sold.

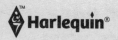

Harlequin®

COMING NEXT MONTH

Available May 10, 2011

#1353 A RANCHER'S PRIDE
American Romance's Men of the West
Barbara White Daille

#1354 THE COWBOY'S TRIPLETS
Callahan Cowboys
Tina Leonard

#1355 SUDDENLY TEXAN
Brody's Crossing
Victoria Chancellor

#1356 THE MARRIAGE SOLUTION
Fatherhood
Megan Kelly

You can find more information on upcoming
Harlequin® titles, free excerpts and more at
www.HarlequinInsideRomance.com.

REQUEST YOUR FREE BOOKS!
2 FREE NOVELS PLUS 2 FREE GIFTS!

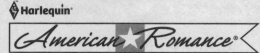

♦ Harlequin®

American ★ Romance®

LOVE, HOME & HAPPINESS

YES! Please send me 2 FREE Harlequin American Romance® novels and my 2 FREE gifts (gifts are worth about $10). After receiving them, if I don't wish to receive any more books, I can return the shipping statement marked "cancel." If I don't cancel, I will receive 4 brand-new novels every month and be billed just $4.24 per book in the U.S. or $4.99 per book in Canada. That's a saving of at least 15% off the cover price! It's quite a bargain! Shipping and handling is just 50¢ per book in the U.S. and 75¢ per book in Canada.* I understand that accepting the 2 free books and gifts places me under no obligation to buy anything. I can always return a shipment and cancel at any time. Even if I never buy another book, the two free books and gifts are mine to keep forever.

154/354 HDN FDKS

Name	(PLEASE PRINT)

Address	Apt. #

City	State/Prov.	Zip/Postal Code

Signature (if under 18, a parent or guardian must sign)

Mail to the **Reader Service:**
IN U.S.A.: P.O. Box 1867, Buffalo, NY 14240-1867
IN CANADA: P.O. Box 609, Fort Erie, Ontario L2A 5X3

Not valid for current subscribers to Harlequin American Romance books.

Want to try two free books from another line?
Call 1-800-873-8635 or visit www.ReaderService.com.

* Terms and prices subject to change without notice. Prices do not include applicable taxes. Sales tax applicable in N.Y. Canadian residents will be charged applicable taxes. Offer not valid in Quebec. This offer is limited to one order per household. All orders subject to credit approval. Credit or debit balances in a customer's account(s) may be offset by any other outstanding balance owed by or to the customer. Please allow 4 to 6 weeks for delivery. Offer available while quantities last.

Your Privacy—The Reader Service is committed to protecting your privacy. Our Privacy Policy is available online at www.ReaderService.com or upon request from the Reader Service.

We make a portion of our mailing list available to reputable third parties that offer products we believe may interest you. If you prefer that we not exchange your name with third parties, or if you wish to clarify or modify your communication preferences, please visit us at www.ReaderService.com/consumerschoice or write to us at Reader Service Preference Service, P.O. Box 9062, Buffalo, NY 14269. Include your complete name and address.

HAR11

*With an evil force hell-bent on destruction,
two enemies must unite to find a truth that turns
all-too-personal when passions collide.*

*Enjoy a sneak peek in Jenna Kernan's next installment
in her original* TRACKER *series, GHOST STALKER,
available in May, only from Harlequin Nocturne.*

"Who are you?" he snarled.

Jessie lifted her chin. "Your better."

His smile was cold. "Such arrogance could only come from a Niyanoka."

She nodded. "Why are you here?"

"I don't know." He glanced about her room. "I asked the birds to take me to a healer."

"And they have done so. Is that *all* you asked?"

"No. To lead them away from my friends." His eyes fluttered and she saw them roll over white.

Jessie straightened, preparing to flee, but he roused himself and mastered the momentary weakness. His eyes snapped open, locking on her.

Her heart hammered as she inched back.

"Lead who away?" she whispered, suddenly afraid of the answer.

"The ghosts. Nagi sent them to attack me so I would bring them to her."

The wolf must be deranged because Nagi did not send ghosts to attack living creatures. He captured the evil ones after their death if they refused to walk the Way of Souls, forcing them to face judgment.

"Her? The healer you seek is also female?"

"Michaela. She's Niyanoka, like you. The last Seer of Souls and Nagi wants her dead."

Jessie fell back to her seat on the carpet as the possibility of this ricocheted in her brain. Could it be true?

"Why should I believe you?" But she knew why. His black aura, the part that said he had been touched by death. Only a ghost could do that. But it made no sense.

Why would Nagi hunt one of her people and why would a Skinwalker want to protect her? She had been trained from birth to hate the Skinwalkers, to consider them a threat.

His intent blue eyes pinned her. Jessie felt her mouth go dry as she considered the impossible. Could the trickster be speaking the truth? Great Mystery, what evil was this?

She stared in astonishment. There was only one way to find her answers. But she had never even met a Skinwalker before and so did not even know if they dreamed.

But if he dreamed, she would have her chance to learn the truth.

Look for GHOST STALKER by Jenna Kernan, available May only from Harlequin Nocturne, wherever books and ebooks are sold.

Love Inspired.
HISTORICAL
INSPIRATIONAL HISTORICAL ROMANCE

Introducing a brand-new
heartwarming Amish miniseries,

AMISH BRIDES
of Celery Fields

Beginning in May with

Hannah's Journey
by ANNA SCHMIDT

Levi Harmon, a wealthy circus owner, never expected to find
the embodiment of all he wanted in the soft-spoken, plainly
dressed woman. And for the Amish widow Hannah Goodloe,
to love an outsider was to be shunned. The simple pleasures
of family, faith and a place to belong seemed an impossible
dream. Unless Levi unlocked his past and opened his heart
to God's plan.

Find out if love can conquer all
in HANNAH'S JOURNEY,
available May wherever books are sold.

INTRIGUE

WILL THE QUEST FOR THE KILLERS BE TOO MUCH FOR THIS TOWN TO HANDLE?

FIND OUT IN THE NEWEST MINISERIES BY *USA TODAY* BESTSELLING AUTHOR

B.J. DANIELS

WHITEHORSE MONTANA

Chisholm Cattle Company

Colton Chisholm has lived with the guilt of not helping his high-school sweetheart when she needed him most. Fourteen years later, he's committed to finding out what happened to her the night she disappeared. The same night he stood her up.

BRANDED

May 2011

Five more titles to follow....

HI69543